HELEN'S STORIES

Foreword

Back in 1995, our sister Joan was dying of cancer. What can you do when something like that falls on a family? Helen had an idea. She would tell Joan stories, recorded on tape, about the days when they were young, back in the 1950s and 60s. She invented a family with the main character being a girl with red hair that she called Angela. Angela was the youngest daughter, but she did have a little brother Bobbie that she was expected to take with her when she least wanted to. And two big sisters, that we shall call Barbara.

In the first story, the family was living in a mixed neighbourhood in an industrial town in Northern Ireland. Later they move to a large house with a big garden when the father becomes Mayor of the town. He is an officer in the territorial army in a regiment filled with landed gentry and a well-known person in the town but the truth is, the family income is very modest and the house was bought at a good price because the neighbourhood was not the best.

The stories capture the problems of living in a community that has fixed values that are in reality, built on illusions. But isn't that the same everywhere?

Time moves on and the stories on tape have a hard time finding a tape recorder to play them. I thought it was time to go back to good old pen and paper and encouraged Helen to type up transcripts of the originals and why not, start to write some more.

Angela grows up and moves to teach in a primary school in the East End of London.

The following stories are about her reminiscences there and the people she meets. Are the stories real, well… let's just say they are authentic. Another community but as always, filled with characters.

I believe that the strain that runs through these stories are that people live and people die but the memory of them lives on. The influence they had on your life. And through telling stories, their lives will go on and on.

I hope you enjoy them and maybe recognize some of these characters, in people you have met and times you have lived.

Brian Mitchell (or maybe Bobbie)

CHILDHOOD

Mammy's Mite

"Is your Mammy in, love?" The voice was plaintive. Standing on the doorstep with her floral pinny wrapped tightly round her was Aggie, an elderly lady from down the road, her face was pale and serious.

"Surely, I'll get her for you now. MAMMY! MAMMY! Aggie's wanting you, she's at the door.

"Stop shouting, Angela There's no need for that, I'm here. Sorry about that Aggie, what can I do for you?"

"It's a bit private Mrs., if you don't mind; but I just didn't know who to turn to"

"Come on in dear, Angela you go and play!"

Mammy took Aggie into the living room and closed the door firmly behind her.

Angela wandered off into the garden with her skipping rope knowing she would have to be careful not to knock the heads off any flowers again as the garden was Daddy's pride and joy. Certainly, everything looked beautiful and so colourful!

Their bungalow was situated on a country lane and every weekend people of the neighbourhood, going for a walk, would stop and admire their garden, remarking on its beauty. From this lane you could walk all the way to the other side of town stopping off perhaps at another spot called "Lover's Lane".

"Thank you so much Mrs. I'll pay you back as soon as I can. Your Mammy's kindness itself so she is!" With this Aggie rushed off through the gate and away. Locally, she was known as a decent wee woman who looked after her old Da and bothered nobody.

As Angela skipped repeating the rhyme" Salt, Mustard, Vinegar, Pepper" over and over again, her little brother Bobbie rode out of the garage on his tricycle.

"When's Daddy coming home? he demanded as Angela finished skipping.

"Now, Bobbie, you know perfectly well!" She put on her exasperated, big sister voice. "You know he is away at the Territorial Army camp for two weeks in England which is a very faraway place. In fact, it is across the sea, and he will be back on Saturday!"

Angela had no idea what Daddy and his friends did at this camp all dressed up in their uniforms, but she knew one thing for sure, he always came back with a present for each of them.

They had all promised to be good and help Mammy as much as possible.

Later that day, while Mammy went into town for some shopping, leaving big sister Barbara in charge, Angela thought she might do something especially good. Looking around, she noticed that something was spoiling the view. Cow Clap! Just outside the gate from John Joe McConville's cows as they were taken to market. What an eyesore, something needed to be done and she was the girl to do it!

A brilliant idea struck her, so simple, make it beautiful!

Getting out her sand bucket and summoning wee Bobbie's help, they set about gathering stones, daisies and a few flower heads. Carefully, very carefully, they surrounded the great dollops of dung with stones and strewed flowers and daisies over the top.

Sitting back on her heels, Angela heaved a sigh of contentment.

"Hurrah! We have made the cow clap beautiful; everyone will be so pleased!"

Bobby chuckled and they went off to wash their hands.

Suddenly, her mood was broken by an angry voice shouting,

"For the love of God, who's responsible for this tomfoolery"?

There, in a heap on the ground, was Jerry McStravick, in his busman's uniform having fallen off his bike!

"What have you done this for, covering up cow clap with stones, causing accidents. Your father will tan your hides for this!"

For goodness's sake, what was the matter with the man, did he prefer looking at cow clap? Obviously, he did, because he ordered Angela to move all the stones, which it has to be said, was not a nice job, plus he stood arms, akimbo, till he was satisfied with the end result. She had tried to explain her vision, but he would have none of it! Bobby and Barbara hid out of the way!

By the time she had finished, Angela decided she would never again try to make the world a lovelier place, just leave it to Daddy, he seemed to know how to please the public, she obviously didn't!

Later that evening, she woke up with a start, sitting up in bed she heard voices, yes, at least two people were talking to Mammy. Oh No! It must be Jerry McStravick and his wife, who came to complain about her!

Cautiously, she crept out of her room and listened at the top of the stairs. There was at least two men and a woman's voice but what they were saying she couldn't work out.

As they came out of the living room, Angela heard:

"I don't know how to thank you. As soon as Billy is back from the camp, we will be round with the money!"

The front door closed, thank goodness, it wasn't anyone from the McStravick clan! Angela climbed back into bed and slept like the proverbial log.

The week passed, everything seemed normal, maybe a bit short of treats, but that wasn't unusual.

Aggie turned up on the Thursday morning and Mammy seemed really pleased to see her.

Saturday morning brought Daddy bounding back, arms full of presents!

"Come on everyone, I've got something for you all!"

No doubt about it, Daddy was an expert at buying presents and England must be a wonderful place, full of shops! Angela gift was the most beautiful doll she had ever seen with hair you could comb and plait! Amazing!

When all the excitement had died down and Angela was ensconced on Daddy's lap, Mammy began to tell him what had happened while he was away.

Poor old Aggie had run into some kind of money problem and needed to borrow the rent but had paid it back. The Johnstons also turned up needing help. Billy Johnston was at camp with Daddy's regiment.

Apparently, the eldest Johnston was a door-to-door salesman and had pretended to have lots of orders with customers who didn't exist. He owed the company money, and his sales manager was going to report him to the police if the family couldn't come up with the cash. With her husband at camp, Mrs. Johnston couldn't think of anyone to help except Mammy. So, she had come round with the man from the company and the errant son begging for money and promising to pay when her husband returned with his TA bonus.

That evening the Johnstons did come up with a fraction of the money and further promises to pay the remainder.

Of course, Angela didn't know about all of this till years later. Strangely enough, the Johnston's borrowed the exact amount that Daddy had left for the two weeks and Aggie had borrowed the equivalent of the Family Allowance! Mammy had lent her all! Her Mite in Biblical terms.

Needless to say, the Johnston's never fully repaid the money they borrowed, obviously honesty didn't run in that family! What Angela could never understand was why the neighbours from both sides of the community came to their house when in need! Maybe it was the magic of the beautiful garden which drew them, who knows? Sure, her family had something to offer the neighbourhood, loving kindness and generosity of spirit.

Years later, when Angela visited that neighbourhood, everyone she met welcomed her in and remembered her parents with real warmth and fond memories. The lady who lived in their old house said that, as a little girl, she had passed it every day and promised herself that when she grew up that would be her home.

The magic lives on!

Dental Care

Angela was deep in knots when her guide leader interrupted, just as she had managed to hoist the flag up the pole! The Guides met after school on a Monday night and Angela was determined to pass this part of the latest badge. She had been practicing at every opportunity. Now, it seemed her mother had phoned to tell her that the receptionist at the dentist had called; Angela was late for her appointment, could she get there as quickly as possible.

Mammy must be joking! Mr. Anderson's surgery was at the top of the High Street, a 40-minute walk and a fast walk at that! You'd need to be Roger Bannister to get there quickly!

As she set off Angela wondered what horrible treatment was in store.

The sky was darkening, a slight drizzle began. Angela's heart sank as she half ran, half walked. A carpet of wet leaves squelched under her school shoes.

The journey took her through the town, past the lights of the shops which were ready for closing. A few last shoppers were making their way home to warm houses and mouthwatering teas.

A stitch pinched in Angela's side, her breath caught and rasped at the back of her throat, sweat broke on her brow and mingling with rain, rolled down her face and dripped under the collar of her raincoat.

At last, the surgery was in sight. Angela could not go any further. Making one last courageous effort, she dragged herself to the door and rang the bell. Standing on the doorstep gasping, riddled with pain from the stitch, her face streaked with rain drenched sweat she must have looked like an orphan from a Dicken's novel.

Miss O'Neil, the receptionist, opened the door, looked at Angela as if she was something a dog had left, and in a voice which froze her blood said,

"I'm very sorry, Mr. Anderson has finished for the day. If you want to make another appointment, please phone!"

The door slammed shut! Angela stared at the brass plate; it couldn't be! She had half killed herself to get there just to be turned away? Hot tears pricked her eyes and joined the sweat and rain.

Right, she thought, if that's the way they want it that's the way it shall be! Old Anderson will never get his rubber gloved hands on her teeth again! Oh No! Never again!

The journey home was taken up by thoughts of how she could get her own back on that snooty old bag and her rotten boss.

On seeing the state she was in, Angela's mother's fury turned on the cruelty of the dentist.

"And to think that man calls himself a Christian! I shall cut him dead when I see him at church on Sunday! May God in his mercy find a suitable punishment for him. The sanctimonious old goat! How could he do that to a twelve-year-old child?"

Angela told her Mammy that she would never go back. She would find a new dentist. One who was kind to children, who understood the frailties of mankind: a dentist worthy of being called by that name!

Two weeks later, Angela remembered why she had needed dental care. A small hole in her upper left molar had improved in size. Helped along, no doubt, by the race she had with her friend Maureen to see who could crunch two ounces of clove rock the quickest! Winning through sheer experience, Angela now squirmed every time anything cold tried to pass her gums!

Noticing Angela's discomfort, Mammy suggested phoning Mr. Anderson for an appointment. Angela couldn't believe her ears! Phone that blackguard! She would rather suffer! How could Mammy forget so quickly? Oh No, she would stick to her guns!

On her way home from school each day, she had noticed a shiny new plate with PJ O'Donnell clearly inscribed. So, at the first opportunity she went in. The premises had previously been run by a Mr. O'Flynn who had died in mysterious circumstances in an Italian police cell.

Inside, at a desk, sat Dymphna McGonagle, a large, freckled girl that Angela knew by sight. She was wearing a white linen coat and politely inquired how she could be of assistance.

Angela, who was also ginger and freckled, saw in Dymphna a sister of mercy. Quickly an appointment was made. Angela departed cheerily, a little white card with the date and time clenched in her hand. The beauty of it was, Mr. O'Donell's surgery was just round the corner from her home. BRILLIANT!

"But Angela dear, he's a Catholic!" Mammy's tones were hushed as if she was being overheard.

"SO!" Angela barked defiantly. "I don't care whether he's a Catholic or a Hindu, so long as he is kind and can do the job!"

"Oh well, whatever you like, pet. Anything for a quiet life"

Angela arrived at the dental surgery in good time. Amazingly there seemed to be lots of people taking up ALL the seats. She didn't recognize any of them.

Smiling nervously, Angela said, "Good afternoon. It's been a grand day, hasn't it?"

That seemed to break the ice.

"Indeed, it is Miss", said a large, cheery faced woman." Sean, get up and give the child your seat. Come on, pet come and sit next to me, sure Sean can sit on my knee".

Soon Angela was privy to the medical and dental history of the lady's entire family. Seven children she had, each one of them appeared to be totally accident prone or prey to every disease known to the Western World!

One by one the patients were seen. Darkness began falling by the time it was Angela's turn. Dymphna apologized for the delay and explained that Mr. O'Donal never turned anyone away.

Entering the surgery Angela heard the gentle burr of a Southern Irish accent.

"Well, hello, you must be Angela, come in, come in! It's lovely to meet you. What can I do for you, today?"

For the first time in her twelve years, Angela was rendered speechless. Mr. O'Donal turn as he spoke. Beautiful blue eyes smiled at her. They were set in a young, extremely handsome face. He looked like a film star! His skin was a golden tan, rarely seen in her town, and his body was enclosed in a white coat the same style as Dr. Kildare on the television: high at the neck and buttoned all down the side.

What needed doing? She couldn't remember!

Again, she heard him speak. "Up in the chair young Angela, open wide, now. There's a good girl."

Whatever he had asked her to do she would have obeyed blindly. The blue eyes were so, so close as he inspected her teeth. Angela recalled reading a soppy love story her friend Maureen had brought to school. How they laughed over the phrase... "eyes like pools you could drown in." Now she realized that such a vision was true!

"There's a good girl now", Mr. O'Donal's voice was soothing.

"Do I need an injection?" her voice sounded strangled.

"Oh now, Angela, would I do that to you?"

Of course, this gorgeous creature wouldn't be capable of doing anything horrible to anyone, although common sense told her he might find it hard to fill such a big cavity without some sort of painkiller.

While she was pondering this, Mr. O'Donal began rubbing ointment on her gum. It was a pleasant sensation and with the blue eyes twinkling, Angela felt her tongue begin to thicken up.

"Now tell me, Angela, what is your best subject at school?"

While trying to form sentences without the use of her tongue, Angela saw a glimpse of metal! God, he had a needle in his hand and was aiming for her gum! Concentrating on his hypnotic eyes and breathing hard, the deed was done! She didn't feel a thing!

The rest of the treatment was filled with reassuring chat and lots of questions she was incapable of answering! Angela was in heaven, sitting with the full attention of this Adonis whispering sweet nothings in her ear.

"I'll need to see you again, Angela, there's a wee bit more work to be done. Is that alright?"

Alright! I'll say it's alright! Thanking him she made an appointment with Dymphna for the next week and floated home.

Mammy ran out of the kitchen, her apron flying, as Angela opened the front door.

"Where have you been, child, it's nearly six o'clock!"

Angela grinned like an idiot. Everything in the house had a rosy glow!

"Oh Mammy, he's gorgeous, just like Dr. Kildare. I had a wonderful time and I'm going back next week!"

For the rest of the evening the whole family were bored to death listening to the wonder and beauty of Mr. Paddy O'Donal!

Well, they may have appeared bored, but two weeks later big sister Barbara just happened to have a problem with a wisdom tooth. Angela spotted her setting off, wearing her newest dress which was very low cut!

Mammy also found the need to pop in, after all, Angela's National Health form had to be signed and she had some painful inflammation of the gums.

In fact, it wasn't long before many ladies, young and old in the town became more dentally aware! Stories were told of Mr. O'Donal being chased round his dentist's chair by matrons seeking some special attention!

Certainly, Angela had no doubt that attending the dentist was one appointment that nobody forgot!

Happy Days!

The idea of toffee apples had come to Bernadette in the middle of the night when she was looking after the youngest child. Now where could she get a supply of good apples?

Every day she passed the big house, unavoidable considering it towered over the neighbourhood. The orchard in the grounds was a favourite place with the local kids, to do a bit of forging/ stealing the apples.

Her plan was to go up, knock on the door and politely offer to buy some apples. It was a daring idea! How should she dress? Respectable and businesslike? After all, she didn't want to be chased off by the dog!

First she fed the two little ones their porridge, then dressed in her mother's go to mass coat and tying her curly long hair into a bun, she set off with her basket on her arm. Her purse held the money she had saved from the housekeeping. Hope it was enough!

There was a gate and a secluded driveway; the walk took all of Bernadette's courage. Suddenly it opened up to reveal the house and the garden. Bernadette gasped at the size of it all. There must be loads of rooms, and the garden was so full of flowers! She had never seen anything like it! They even had their own tennis court and what was that beyond the lawn? A pony no less, kicking up its heels. God, there was everything here, large trees with birds squawking in them, green lawns and roses growing over an archway.

No cars were parked in front of the house! Now Bernadette knew the family had two cars: one for the man and one for the woman. Imagine that! A woman having her own car! It was just a little red one, but it could go really fast. She had seen the eldest girl driving it, all dressed up, hair piled on her head, bright red lipstick on her lips. Bernadette wasn't sure about painted faces, part of her longed to be glamorous while part of her thought she should be as God made her.

Her heart was pounding as she walked up the steps and knocked on the large imposing front door. The sound echoed through the house, and it seemed ages before anyone answered, but at last it opened a fraction and a young face, framed by lots of ginger hair, peered round it.

Bernadette recognized her, it was the younger daughter of the family who she had seen in Flynn's butcher shop.

The door opened wider. The girl's smile was friendly,

"Hello there! What can I do for you?"

Bernadette spoke in her best convent voice,

"I believe you have some apples to sell"

The girl looked confused,

"Well, we do have apples!"

"I would like to purchase some of them, how much do they cost?"

The girl's face became business like,

"Right, let's go and have a look and see what you want"

She led Bernadette round to the back of the house where there were several buildings and walked into one, which smelled sweetly of apples.

The girl was dressed in a pair of tight blue jeans and a baggy sweater, her hair was very ginger. I bet she gets teased a lot, thought Bernadette.

Just then a large dog bounded into the barn, barking loudly.

"Don't take any notice of this soppy old thing, he's jealous of the new arrivals! One of our cats has had a litter of kittens and he doesn't like anyone making a fuss of them, do you, boy?"

Bernadette looked down and saw a mother cat washing several little tabby kittens. They were so sweet!

"You wouldn't like a kitten as well, would you?" asked the girl, hopefully.

Bernadette imagined bringing home another mouth to feed!

"Not at the moment," she answered politely.

"Right, let's have a look at these apples. What do you want them for? And how many do you need?"

"I want to make toffee apples and sell them. I want half a crown's worth".

"What a brilliant idea!" exclaimed the girl, "I love toffee apples! You will need our best ones! We don't want any dissatisfied customers, do we?"

Soon her basket was full of beautiful apples.

"Are you sure you can manage; I could help you carry them home?"

The girl was being helpful, but Bernadette just wanted to get on with her project.

She handed over the money and set off.

"Don't forget, if you want any more you know where to come!" Shouted the girl. "Goodbye and good luck!"

Bernadette hugged herself, what a bargain. She hoped the girl wouldn't get into trouble selling the apples so cheaply. In her head she calculated how much profit she could make. Perhaps there would be enough to treat herself to a lipstick from

Woolworth's store in the town. Certainly, the money she hoped to make would be a start to her fund. She giggled with pleasure and anticipation.

....
....

The weekend had got off to a bad start for Angela. First Daddy said IF no one was going to look after the pony properly, he was going to return it to its owner. To be honest, none of them had really wanted a pony. It had been a novelty to start with, but really it needed far too much attention. You rode it for ten minutes, brushed it down, cleaned the saddle and bit etc. for an hour! Who wanted to do that?

Next, the apples they had spent ages gathering in, so that the neighbourhood couldn't steal them, were another headache. I mean Mammy could only make SO much apple jelly!

Then, on top of it all, Angela's sister had taken herself off in Mammy's car without saying when she would be back! That meant that their trip to the Chinese Restaurant in Belfast was on hold!

Opening the door to Bernadette and getting rid of some of the apples brightened up Angela's day! She looked at the half-crown! Great! Now she could buy that lipstick in Woolworth's, the one that was all the rage "Kissable Pink" it was called.

"Angela, darlin? How much did you get for the apples?"

Oh no! Mammy must have seen the exchange from the window!

She showed her mother the money.

"Now Angela pet, can you just pop up to the butcher's and buy a pound of sausages for our tea. If there's any money over, buy yourself some wee thing!"

Angela was good at knowing the price of meat as she was a regular at Flynn's shop. She had recognized Bernadette from the last time she was there.

Getting the lipstick was first on her agenda so she nipped into Woolworth's and couldn't believe her luck! Kissable Pink was on special offer and half price! Yippee, things were looking up! After paying for it she went to the part of the store which sold mirrors and tried it on! Gosh! It was glossy. Now to Flynn's butcher's shop.

The eldest boy Flynn had gone to be a priest and the second son Paddy worked in the shop. He was well known as a boxer for his local club and was gorgeous, with rippling muscles, black curly hair and always a cheeky smile on his face. He must be seventeen, if a day, and loved to tease all the girls.

"Well, Carrot tops, what can we do for you this fine day?"

Angela rubbed her lips together and pouted a little as she had seen in a film.

"A pound of your best sausages, please, Paddy"

"Is that lipstick you've got on, you young monkey? Your Daddy will be after you for that, so he will" and he laughed loudly.

"Oh really, Paddy" she said patronizingly, "It's 1959 you know, not the Dark Ages! Anyway, I'm nearly fifteen!"

"Sorry, Madam, I didn't realize I was talking to a grown up!"

Angela took the sausages and her change and walked out of the shop giggling. Paddy was such a laugh, he always cheered her up.

Now, back to Woolworth's to spend what was left on some sweets! Happy Days!

....
....

Bernadette was delighted. She had been right! The local children flocked to buy the toffee apples. By half past three she had sold out, cleared up and counted all the pennies and half pennies. Her fund was off to a good start!

But first she would pop out to Woolworth's and buy herself something as a treat, something just for herself! She was thrilled when she saw the "Kissable Pink" lipstick on special offer! What a bit of luck!

Back home she tried it on and combed her hair out. Yes, it was just the thing, very glossy, very sophisticated!

Her father's voice called her back from her daydreams.

"Well, young lady, I believe you have been making yourself a wee fortune today. No doubt you'll be giving us all a treat. Fish suppers all round, I think, hey, kids?"

Her brothers and sisters all squealed with delight and pulled at her skirts.

"YES, YES, Bernie! Chips, Chips"

Looking at their little faces, full of hope, well, what else could she do?

"Aye, alright, I won't be long, get the table set!"

Swinging her hair back, Bernadette rubbed her glossy lips together and walked smartly to O'Brian's fish and chip shop. There wouldn't be much of her toffee apple money left, perhaps she had been too reckless with buying the lipstick. Her fund was off to a very small start.

As she stood in the queue a familiar voice spoke into her ear.

"Hello there!"

Turning abruptly her face almost touched that of Paddy Flynn. He smiled,

"I see lipstick is all the rage today!"

"Well, maybe it is, after all its 1959 and I'm nearly sixteen, so why wouldn't I be wearing lipstick on a Saturday night?"

He waited and walked up the street with her.

"Well, maybe a grown-up young lady would like to come to the pictures with me next week?"

Blushing, she looked at his twinkling, blue eyes and curly black hair and accepted his invitation.

Seeing her to her door he said,

"I'll call for you on Tuesday at seven o'clock, and don't forget the lipstick!"

Her father had been watching.

"Well young Bernadette, now his brother has gone for the priesthood, Paddy will be in line to take over the butcher's. With your business sense you two could make a grand pair!"

Maybe, thought Bernadette to herself, whatever way you look at it, that lipstick was a sound investment. Happy Days!

Eggs is Eggs

Angela wiped each egg carefully as she knew they had to be perfectly dry, otherwise they would go bad. It was a goodly collection this time, her hens were really good layers. Putting them into her basket she heard her Mammy call.

"Hurry up Angela, they will be closing soon, and make sure you get a fair price for them!"

Angela knew she would NOT be haggling with Mr. O'Kane of Armstrong's Chicken Packing Company, she would accept whatever he offered! It was humiliating enough, so it was selling eggs, Mammy ought to try it sometime!

She put on her regulation school raincoat. Wearing school uniform made her feel younger and more pathetic when she went to Armstrong's, not that anyone there ever treated her badly. Quite the opposite, they were all very kind.

How did the egg business start? Well, a few months previously, Daddy had helped one of his friends out of a fix and as a repayment he had given Daddy some chickens!

These little chicks started producing more eggs than their family could eat, so Maggie, their cleaner and all-round encyclopaedia, suggested that the surplus could be sold to Armstrong's. This would pay for their keep! Genius! Of Course, who was going to do the deal? As usual, it fell to Angela, the family peacekeeper! However, it had turned out in her favour as she negotiated a percentage of any money made from the sale for herself! She wasn't that big of a mug!

What tickled her about the whole transaction was that recently, after counting heads, the number of chickens had grown! The extra ones had escaped from Armstrong's, which was nearby, and flown over the hedge to join her merry band! She was now selling THEM eggs from THEIR own hens. Righteous justice as they were helping to pay for their food!

Armstrong's was an American company with strict rules of employment. Notices about this were on the noticeboard of the office, especially about employing people with handicaps. Now everyone in their town knew that no matter what good intentions employers had, there was no way mixing religions worked. So, Angela was aware that all the staff in Armstrong's were Catholics.

Until Maggie had come to work for them, Angela had been totally ignorant about the differences between Catholics and Protestants. Now, Maggie had filled in some of the gaps! You see her niece, Aileen, was married to a man who "dug with the other foot" she explained in hushed tones. Aileen had unsuspectedly travelled in a closed railway carriage all the way to Belfast with a Catholic male and had succumbed to his charms.

Maggie warned Angela to be on her guard at Armstrong's as it was full of red-blooded youths. Thus, the school uniform which Angela wore should help to keep them at bay!

Certainly, there was one tall, dark-haired guy called Sean, who always ceremoniously escorted Angela to the egg department.

"Well, here's Miss Angela, all the way from the big house, come to visit us. And what would you have in your basket today, Miss? Would it be eggs now? Well, well, isn't that lovely! Let me take you to Bernie the Beautiful!"

He would take her hand, his hand always felt cold and clammy, not surprising as he spent his days loading up the deep freeze. However, he was very good-looking, no doubt about that, a little bit like Elvis in a Teddy Boy way. He would take her basket in a gentlemanly way and twirl her under his arm. This made Angela blush to the roots of her hair. The last time she was there he bowed to her and said,

"Before I hand you over to the lovely Bernie, I would like to present you with a small token as a respected customer."

Out of his pocket he took a furry object, Angela's eyes widened, it was a rabbit's foot! At school, this was the latest craze! Now she had one, thanks Sean!

"They're supposed to be lucky, young Miss, though the rabbit wasn't too fortunate, was he?"

Sean burst into peals of laughter and all the workers around joined in.

"Now, Bernie, me darling, take good care of this wee girl! See you soon again, now!"

He said something in the Irish language which Angela didn't understand and walked away.

Bernadette looked after his disappearing form with a strange look in her eyes.

"He's a caution," laughed Angela," and so handsome!"

"Handsome is as handsome does!" Bernadette replied sharply. "That young man should watch himself!"

Bernadettes's face looked hard, and her eyes glittered.

"Now, love, what little goodies have you got for me today?"

Bernadette was Angela's favourite egg checker. She must have been about twenty, with brown curly hair covered by a hygienic net and had a really lovely smile and usually was very cheerful and warm. Selling eggs was a humiliating experience, but Bernadette and Sean, plus all the others in company, made Angela feel welcome, even a bit special. It wasn't too bad really, not when you actually got there. Also, Angela had never had an egg fail the test when Bernadette put each one in turn under a lamp and then sent them on their way. All her eggs were perfect!

Bernadette would give Angela a piece of paper, a chitty, with the number of eggs to take to the office and claim her cash! The very best bit!

Each time Angela went to the office window she was excited to see how much the eggs were, as it changed week to week. While she waited for Mr. O'Kane to count out the money, she saw other notices. One that always caught her eye showed the percentage of people employed with handicaps. She never saw that information anywhere else.

Little did she know that her trips to Armstrong's would come to a sudden end!

When she got home, she discovered that all hell had broken loose! While she was out, their dog had got in among the chickens and had killed two of them. Daddy had given him a thorough thrashing. Mammy was crying and wringing her hands. The rest of the family were nowhere to be seen!

Daddy was demented! That was it, he said, the hens would have to go before the dog killed them all! Sure enough, next morning he arranged for Armstrong's to come and collect the remaining hens and they took the carcasses as well. The end of an era! An Egg era!

Angela was sorry to see them go but also upset about the dog, who had been jealous of the hens and made a big fuss every time she fed them. Now what was she going to do for money? Thank goodness she had saved a lot of the egg money. Certainly, she had learned a financial lesson! DON'T COUNT ON YOUR CHICKENS!

One Sunday morning, several weeks later, Mammy had discovered that they had run out of mustard powder. This would mean a volcanic eruption from Daddy as he couldn't possibly eat his dinner without mustard! As usual, Angela came to the rescue. She knew from past experience which shops in the Catholic estate were open on a Sunday, Protestant shops never were.

She ran down to Jimmy's, a shop which appeared to be open all day, every day. There was quite a queue: Other families, no doubt with temperamental fathers!

As she waited, she overheard a conversation. It was about a young man found face down in a ditch with a bullet in the back of his head. Seemingly, he had been a bit of a lothario. Apparently, he had been playing fast and loose with a cripple girl, an egg checker at Armstrong's whose father and brother were "Big Men" in the organization, and everyone knew what that was!

 Worse, though, he had Talked!

Angela's heart froze! The description fitted Sean. God help us all! Surely not! Could the girl be Bernadette, was she a cripple? Angela had never seen her walking. She couldn't ask in the shop as people would wonder why she was so nosy.

Maggie, of course, knew all about it. Yes, Sean was your man! He had got friendly with young Bernadette on a works outing to the seaside, they were in the same carriage on a train. Angela felt terrible, she had liked the couple, now to think of him and poor Bernadette, more casualties of the railway system.

Handsome is as handsome does, Bernadette had said, Angela had never understood that saying until now. She looked at the rabbit's foot Sean had given her. Lucky for nobody! Perhaps he should have kept it! She took it down to the garden and ceremoniously buried it where the hens had run about. A chapter of her life was over! It was all too Tragic!

As she looked in the mirror that night her face looked older and wiser. God preserve us all! It must be a fearsome responsibility being an adult! Right now, she didn't know how she would cope with romance, when it came. If it came?

Mind you she might end up an old maid, living in a cottage, looking after chickens. Well maybe that would be the safest thing to do, at least she was experienced in that field!

A Chinese Cracker

Angela groaned, it was Sunday, the most boring day of the week! At least she had persuaded her mother that afternoon Bible Class wasn't for her. Before that Sunday was just a round of Church, Sunday School and Church again! Deadly dull!

Daddy went every other week to visit his mother in far flung Co. Antrim and little brother, Bobby, the son and heir went with him. While they were gone, Mammy and Angela had found a new way to pass the time: drive to Belfast, to the Peacock Restaurant and thence partake of some exotic Chinese Food!

It didn't take much to persuade Mammy to go, as long as the Northern Ireland weather was on your side, sadly not always the case. First Mammy had to have a lie down after cooking Sunday Dinner, Angela settled down in front of the TV for some culture when later she would waken Mammy with a refreshing cup of tea.

Once they had titivated themselves sufficiently, off they would set, in the good old Mini, on the road to the bright lights! Yes. Chinese food had given Mammy a new lease of life. Here they were, dressed up, hair combed, a drop of Midnight in Paris behind their ears heading towards a culinary feast.

Parking the car outside the Peacock, they walked with light tread towards the delicious aroma. As they approached the door, out came a man, woman and two children.

"Good evening, Mrs. Anderson, Good evening, Angela"

Oh No! It was the McAvoy family from home!

Angela pushed her very flustered mother on into the restaurant and manoeuvred her to a table.

"Trust us to walk into them, and on a Sunday, whatever will they think of us and just at time for the evening service?"

Mammy was looking disappointed but before the edge was taken off, Angela reminded her that the Mc Avoy's had also been to the restaurant and there was no way they would be at the Church either.

This realization cheered Mammy up, especially after having a good look round and not finding any other familiar faces. Now they could get down to enjoying some of their favourite Chinese food. Angela's taste buds were tingling!

Later as they drove home, Mammy took up the McAvoy saga, bemoaning the fact that if they had been ten minutes later, they wouldn't have met up. For goodness' sake, thought Angela, who gives a hoot about the McAvoy's, there's more important things to think about than those dreary people. I mean they looked as miserable as sin!

The weeks passed and nothing could persuade Mammy, on a Sunday to go on a Chinese outing. In fact, after her fright with the McAvoy's, she started to attend the evening service, dragging Angela along for company! Blasted people! Mr. McAvoy was an elder at their church and Mammy must have been hoping to reassure him of her piety!

The McAvoy's had a shop in the High Street and sold a variety of items, toys, stationery and books. Teddy McMahon at school kept saying he was going to ask old McAvoy if he had a copy of Lady Chatterley's Lover, which had just been banned, to see the expression on his face. Angela knew Teddy McMahon was just a mouth on legs and wouldn't have the guts to do anything so ridiculous, however it did make her giggle.

All their church's Sunday School prizes were purchased from the McAvoy's shop, always something respectable, no D H

Lawrence. Mrs. McAvoy worked in the shop with her husband, a nice, quiet wee woman, nearly always dressed in brown, no makeup but a pleasant face.

Bobby, her wee brother, was friendly with their older son, Simon, and the last time he came to their house to play Angela found him tear stained and sobbing. Her first reaction was to blame Bobby, but it turned out that the poor little chap was worried about his parents constantly arguing. When Angela had settled him down, he blurted out that three months earlier, his father had been to a Book fair in London and since then he had been back and forth to England like a yoyo.

His mother had found long blonde hairs on his clothes and had issued an ultimatum; choose his family or THIS WOMAN!

The poor little boys had tried to intervene by leaving notes in the father's bedroom begging him not to leave them. But all was to no avail, it was like he was possessed, there was no reasoning with him, he was prepared to sacrifice all of them to this brazen hussy!

Confession seemed to help calm Simon down and after a glass of lemonade he was in better shape when his mother came to pick him up. Before he left, he asked them not to tell anyone. Mrs. McAvoy didn't get out of the car but shouted her thanks for having Simon.

Later that evening, when her Parents were arguing over the telephone bill and who had made what phone call, Angela felt totally exasperated. For goodness's sake her father's company would pay the bill, if they knew what other people in their town were going through, they should count their blessings!

It must have been the first Monday of the month when the fat hit the fire! The news ran round the town faster than John Joe's greyhound. Mrs. McAvoy and the boys had gone to her parents in the country! McAvoy had installed his mistress in the shop! This kind of carry on didn't happen in their wee town. It might have gone unnoticed in London! What kind of harlot chases a mother and her children out of their own home, it was inconceivable, unbelievable. Not only that, but this Deliah has also changed her surname to McAvoy!!

The whole town was buzzing at this outrage. Wives went through their husbands' clothes looking for signs of debauchery! Husbands checked their alibis for every occasion. Elderly spinsters congratulated themselves that they had never been foolish enough to marry, widows were relieved that their husbands had gone to the grave unblemished.

Everybody watched their Neighbours like hawks but most of all everyone wanted to have a look at the scarlet woman!

Even Angela, sickened by what had happened to the children, couldn't resist the urge to look in the shop window and see this blonde bombshell who had wreaked havoc in their community.

Having no luck, she decided to enter the den of iniquity, knowing that her mother would love to hear all the details even though she wouldn't step foot in the place herself. Needing some ink for her fountain pen, she opened the door!

Strangely enough, old McAvoy looked exactly the same! Certainly, he showed no interest in serving her: no change there, too busy with a rep from a stationery company.

"Can I help you?"

Angela heard an unfamiliar accent spoken by a middle aged frumpy looking woman with fair hair scrapped back into a chignon. Her clothes were shades of fawn, jumper, blouse, skirt. Angela asked for the ink, royal blue, and looked around for the husband thief, who should be lounging against the counter painting her nails, earrings dangling, wearing a tight black dress, luridly smiling a welcome to all and sundry. But there was no sign of her. Probably too lazy, lying on a settee upstairs eating chocolate or peeling a grape.

"Here you are, love"

 The fawn woman handed her the ink, Angela paid and with another look around, she left no wiser than when she went in. This frowsy looking female must be a relative maybe even the floosy's mother.

On reporting back to Mammy, Angela was surprised to discover that the FAWN woman was McAvoy's fancy piece. Angela wasn't convinced; no one would break up their family for her! She was far too ordinary! No Way!

It was true! McAvoy had swopped a brown woman for a fawn one. There was no understanding older people!

However, what was understood was that McAvoy was setting a bad example to all the males of the town. The church removed him as an elder and their business from the shop. Men were warned off associating with him, and women stayed away in case he had developed an appetite. Within three months, McAvoy and his Jezebel were forced to leave the town and flee to England.

The children, as usual, were the ones to suffer most, it seemed the boys were sent off to boarding school, paid for by their Grandad. Bobby had a Christmas card from Simon, just best wishes, no other information.

Back at school, Teddy McMahon explained his theory that old man McAvoy had indeed been corrupted by books like Lady Chatterley's' lover, maybe the experts were right to ban it? Maybe the pen is mightier than marriage vows. Who knows?

Whatever the cause, there was one side effect that suited Angela down to the ground! Mammy was back on the Sunday night trail to the Chinese restaurant. As Mammy said,

" What's the point of running to church on a Sunday, pretending to be so holy, and living in sin the rest of the week?"

"Who's for chicken fried rice?"

Happy Christmas

After counting out her Christmas fund for the third time, Angela could not achieve a higher total. OK it will have to be Woolworth's again this year for family presents.

While walking through her hometown and tuning into the carols coming from the Christmas tree in front of the parish Church, Angela anticipated another celebration with mixed feelings. Now what were the plans for this year?

Christmas Eve would bring Uncle Harry, Auntie Susan and their children. Uncle Harry was a caution! He had a really great sense of humour, not that Angela always understood it. Like at Halloween, what was it he said that made all the grown-ups laugh? Something about the funeral of a woman in the next town where only certain customers could walk behind the hearse. It made no sense, but everyone laughed.

Every time Uncle Harry came over, they all enjoyed his company. Daddy and he talked cars: Harry always had some huge new expensive looking model. He had pots of money and wasn't tight about sharing it. Before he left, he would slip Angela a pound note! Goodness, you could do a lot with that amount of money!

Christmas Day was Church in the morning, a large and delicious Christmas Dinner with all the trimmings and then a ceremonial opening of the pile of presents from the overflowing tea chest in the drawing room. Hopefully she had dropped enough hints about the dress in Harrison's window that even Mammy couldn't get it wrong this year!

Boxing day brought Granny and Uncle Peter plus the dreaded couple, Mammy's sister Madge and her husband George! They belonged to some religious sect which seemed to allow no fun in life.

The problem was they argued all the time! Every visit began with Auntie Madge asking to speak to Mammy in private. Then poor old Daddy would have to listen to George's side of things. All too embarrassing!

By now Angela had arrived at Woolworth's. No doubt her old Sunday School's friend, Frances Brown would be at her usual place, the sweet counter. Francis had shared some tales about how the female staff had to avoid the amorous advances of the manager Mike McKinley. This was astounding to Angela as he was nothing to look at but was married to Miriam O'Neil, an exotic beauty, jet black hair, well groomed, the latest fashion adorning the perfect figure.

Angela took a keen interest in all this as Miriam's younger brother, Timothy, was one of the best-looking boys at the Technical College. Admiring him from afar was all Angela had been able to do but Annette Richardson, when dropping off Angela's invitation, had let on that he was invited to her New Year's Eve party at the Masonic Hall.

Well! With her new dress, a drop of sister Bárbara's Midnight in Paris and a large helping of good luck, anything could happen!

Frances was busy as usual but still managed to pass on some gossip. It seemed that Doreen Gough had got the job of supervisor and had come out of Mike McKinley's office looking flushed, with her hair all over the place and the top button of her blouse undone! Honestly it was like Sodom and Gomorrah at Woolworth's; Angela was glad she was only a customer!

Fortune smiled on her, and the money managed to stretch too, nail polish for Barbara, Matchbox toy for brother Bobby, a tie pin with a pearl on it for Daddy and a bar of smelly soap for Mammy. There was even enough for two ounces of Dolly mixtures and thanks to Frances, a generous two ounces, for herself! Result!

Christmas day came and went. Thank God Mammy had got the right dress! That was one major hurdle over. Sister Barbara has turned up trumps with a bottle of Midnight in Paris! From Bobby, bought by Mammy, of course, a lipstick but not just any old lipstick, it was the latest shade, Golden Chance, very creamy and with an incandescent glow!

Uncle Harry had passed over a pound note, so now she would be able to afford to get her hair styled for the New Year's Eve party. Everything was coming together very nicely!

Boxing Day began well. Grandma and Uncle Peter arrived in good time. There was no sign of Uncle George and Auntie Madge by the time Mammy had the dinner ready: it wasn't like them to miss a free meal.

By One thirty, Daddy decided they could wait no longer. As everyone took their place round the dining room table, the phone rang. Barbara answered it and came in looking concerned. It was Auntie Madge and she wanted to speak to Mammy.

Mammy rushed out to the hall. Daddy made a crack about another lover's quarrel, no doubt. This made everyone laugh heartily. They were all enjoying the joke when Mammy came in looking pale!

"He's Gone!" She said. "George dropped dead this morning, a massive heart attack, the doctor said!"

The room went horribly silent. What a shock! After all he probably wasn't all that old, was he? How awful!

Angela tried to look on the bright side:

"Well, they never got on, always rowing"

Everybody looked at her in horror.

"There's no need for that now, Angela," her mother sounded tearful.

Dinner was finished with reminiscences about what a wonderful man George had been and how much Madge would miss him!

Funerals have always been arranged quickly in Northern Ireland and during the discussion of dates, it suddenly donned on Angela that she might not be able to go to the New Year's Eve party so soon after a family bereavement! Oh No! Mind you, he wasn't a blood relation, she would just have to wait and see!

Surprisingly, for once, events turned out in Angela's favour. Uncle George's religious sect was so exclusive that only male members of it could attend the funeral.

Madge was being comforted by ladies of the sect and Mammy felt totally left out. Not only that: apparently, she planned to sell up and move to a smart part of Belfast. What a surprise!

By the end of December, George was dead and buried with his widow preparing for a completely new life, well away from the rest of the family.

Mammy's hurt feelings at not being needed by her sister, frequently vented themselves into tirades. During one of these outbursts, Angela cautiously brought up the subject of the New Year's Eve party.

She held her breath and waited for the explosion!

Amazingly, Mammy said:

"And why wouldn't you go, Angela? George never missed a party in his life, especially if someone else was paying. You're only young once, you go and enjoy yourself!"

Great! Angela slipped off to have her hair done at Maisie McGee's hair salon, returning with the latest in "Haute Coiffeur".

Later that evening as she danced cheek to cheek with Timothy O'Neil, she just knew that life couldn't get any better, this was going to be a great new year, no mistake!

Of course, Timothy shared his dancing expertise with most of the girls in turn, leaving the last dance to a more mature partner and previous girlfriend.

Angela knew she would never have been allowed to go out with him even if he had asked as she was too young, AND he was from the wrong side of the town.

However, he had said she was very light on her feet! What a beautiful thing to say! That would keep her smiling for a long time to come.

Twelve o'clock chimed and everyone shouted;

HAPPY NEW YEAR TO US ALL!

And it was a happy year! Auntie Madge bought a lovely bungalow in the outskirts of Belfast and took on the mantle of widowhood with relish. She and Mammy reconciled and had lots of good times together in the city.

As for Angela? Well, she had lots of opportunities to put her light feet into action as they spent Easter and Christmas at their house in Portrush with the Arcadia Dance Hall offering daily dances with top Show bands playing the latest music.

If she had learned anything from Uncle George's demise, it was that life was for the living!

Ruby

All the jobs that had to be done were done. The baby fed, her brain damaged sister cleaned up and fed. It was heart breaking how happy the poor soul was to see everyone, smiling and wriggling with happiness, unable to speak or function thanks to a drunken doctor with forceps, held in hands that shook. Kept in a darkened room like a sinful secret, yet so happy and so loved.

She dressed carefully in her school uniform; it had been so thrilling when her father said she could go to the Quaker School and, best of all, as a boarder!

The uniform was specially made for her and she wore it with pride, especially when she was at home. She loved to walk round the town where everyone knew them, as her father owned the Foundry providing work for many families. Her chance to show off! She hadn't many chances to show off as they belonged to the brethren sect so hair and clothes had to conform to the endless ways of keeping the devil at bay!

How she loved the freedom at school, all the subject they did were so interesting. Then there was tennis, how she adored playing tennis! She had made good friends at the school plus she was out from the shadow of her older bossy sister!

Father had assured her that he had put enough money into a bank which would cover her fees until she could have her dream of becoming a teacher. It was all she ever wanted and could picture herself being the kind of teacher she admired.

Walking round and round the park, she tried to make sense of why her world had come crashing down, shattering all those dreams. Last week she had received a letter from home telling her to pack everything and be ready for her father to pick her up.

It was the end of term, but not the end of the year so why did she have to bring everything?

Father sat her down in the Parents room and explained as clearly as he could. There had been a really big Strike, a National strike. People were refusing to work until they got better pay and working conditions. But what had that to do with her?

Because of the strike, the iron and steel which he needed to keep the Foundry going and fulfil their orders was not being produced. However, the men needed paying so that their families could survive. Noone knew how long this strike would last.

With tears in his eyes, he said he had tried so hard to keep going but alas he would need to take the money out of the bank which had been set aside for her education and use it for the men's wages. As a Christian and owner of the Foundry he had to look after his men. When things improved, she could return to school.

Sitting now on one of the benches in the park, she could really let the floodgates open. Sobbing and sobbing she railed at those strikers who had robbed her of an education. Inside herself she knew that she would never return to the school, there was no way back! All she could look forward to was a life of drudgery at home where there were so many needy people and an endless round of household chores.

It was so unfair! Her older sister had had a full education and a job in the Foundry office! Without a full education she gazed into a future like that of her old aunts whose young men had been killed in the war, helping to bring up other family members' children.

Now her eyes felt raw from all the weeping and she knew that her face was flushed. Heaving one last sob, she got up to leave but was stopped in her tracks by the sight of her next-door

Neighbour. Oh No! She was wearing the uniform of a private, very prestigious girls' school. What could she say to her, would she lie? Truthfully, she had no right to be wearing HER uniform anymore.

 AS she turned to walk in the opposite direction, she heard the girl call her name. They sat down on the bench and through copious tears the girl poured out her heart. Sadly, her father's business was on the point of collapse due to this national strike and although she was wearing her school uniform, he could no longer afford for her to go back to the school!

More tears were shed, the girls sat their holding hands in their joint grief. Life seemed hopeless but at least they were not alone. They promised to meet up from time to time and comfort each other, perhaps swop a book or two that they both enjoyed and watch tennis matches in the park during the summer.

Ruby made a solemn promise to herself, if she was fortunate enough to meet a good man, marry and have children, she would make sure that no matter what happened, they would be given every opportunity and support to have a full education.

And readers, she was true to her word!

LATER STORIES

Men from the East

Believe it or not I had never seen anyone with a brown skin before my eldest sister turned up one Saturday afternoon with not just one brown skinned man but three! Plus, one was wearing a very white turban!

My parents had been persuaded to invite these strangers for a visit to a typical Northern Ireland home by our sister, who was a student at Queen's University in Belfast. How she got to know them I'm not too sure. What I did know was that one of them had taken some very flattering photos of her. Also, I noticed that they were older than anyone else she had invited previously.

Now, you need to know that we lived in an old Georgian Rectory set in three acres of land. Our father was an extraordinary gardener, so the grounds consisted of a tennis court, a putting green, a paddock, a Victorian walled garden and a field. Pride of place were colourful, seasonal flower beds and copious sweet-smelling roses growing up and over pergolas. To be honest, it was a paradise, not at all typical of a Northern Ireland family home: probably why my sister wanted to show it off.

Our parents were extremely hospitable and welcomed these unusual guests warmly. The introductions helped us to understand that the gentlemen were from India. One was Hindu, one Sikh and one Muslim: probably, as I learned in later years, not a common mix in their homeland!

My mother was delighted with the Sikh when he explained that his turban was an important part of his religion. She loved the idea that he spoke about his beliefs so freely.

"An example to us all, we Christians should be as proud as he is, speaking up about our beliefs!" She berated us from time to time.

Of course, It did help that he was extremely good looking and attentive to Mammy. She could never resist a handsome charmer: well, she did marry our father!

After a tour around the grounds in beautiful weather and a delicious homemade meal, we learned more about these men. What I do remember was that they were graduate students at the university and the Hindu and Sikh had wives who were still in India. They were all professionals, one a doctor the other two were dentists: in Northern Ireland for a year or so completing further education courses.

In later years, I was a teacher in East London and worked with children and staff from all over the world. From this I learned that Asians are very hospitable, like many Irish people, and love to invite you to their homes. Thus, it was no surprise that the gentlemen from the East were very keen for us to sample some of their Asian cooking and invited us to visit them in Belfast. A date was arranged.

It was a bit of a squeeze in the small upstairs flat where a feast was laid out before us. What I remember most is the poppadums! They were incredible, like really large crisps, freshly fried. The vegetable curry was new to our palate but very tasty and not at all hot. Bless their hearts they provided us with lots of cut up Swiss roll! Someone must have told them that Irish families enjoyed them. They were so kind and made absolutely sure that we were well fed and attended to. It was a lovely, memorable experience!

A couple of years later, when I was a new student in Belfast, I realized that I was passing the house where we had been entertained. It was a cold afternoon, and I knew very few people. Taking a chance, I tentatively rang the bell. The door was opened by the Sikh, who had visited us. He was delighted to see me and welcomed me in to meet his wife who had come over from India to join him.

They treated me like a long-lost family member, making sure I was comfortable and warm and insisted that I stay for afternoon tea. They were so warm and kind that I was quite overwhelmed.

I meant, as likely as not even promised, to visit again, but like most teenagers, I got caught up in my new life as a student and sadly forgot all about them.

The Muslim man took lots of photos of their visit to our home, I never saw any of them, but I do remember him saying, quite sternly, as he pointed his camera,

"Moisten your lips!"

This obviously made a difference and a tip for the future!

Over the years we had a variety of guests at our home, some more memorable than others. Certainly, the Men from the East, are very near the top of the list!

Lizzie

Lizzie pulled a thin cardigan round her scrawny chest, as she stood behind the lamppost watching; her eyes bright, holding back tears. A heavy cough convulsed her undernourished body as thick green phlegm rose up her throat and into her mouth. Quickly, she spat it into the gutter. Her face tightened as she saw three girls all dressed up knock at the door of number 27, the home of her best friend Isadora Quirke. She recognized Maisie, wearing white socks, Josie, carrying a paper bag, and Daisy with a pink ribbon tied into her long black hair. All dressed up for Isadora's birthday party! A party! No one in their street ever had birthday parties. They were lucky if anyone remembered that they had a birthday!!

Families were big in the East End of London; few even had a whole house to themselves. Lizzies' dad was lucky if he had a full week at the docks: if it wasn't for her mother cleaning railway carriages at night the kids would have gone to bed hungry more night's than they did.

Isadora Quirke was different from all the other girls in the street. First of all, they had a whole house to themselves even though Isadora was an only child. People said they had moved into their area after their son had died. Secondly, Isadora had pink cheeks and was so pretty. Lizzie couldn't believe that she wanted to be friends with her; and yet no invitation to her party?

Maisie had bragged about the party at school the previous week.

"Have you been invited, Lizzie, seeing as you say Isadora is YOUR best friend?" she sneered.

"I haven't made up my mind, yet", she stammered.

Josie joined in" Well I'm going, and I've got a present to take with me! Daisy's going too! We're all invited! Look! This came through my door this morning" She held out a small card with hearts in each corner and in neat writing it said;

"Miss Isadora Quirke invites you to her birthday party on Friday at 5 o'clock."

Lizzie's heart leapt; it was the most beautiful thing she had ever seen.

Maybe she had been sent one and her little brothers had got hold of it! Isadora would never have left her out, especially as the other girls weren't really her friends, certainly not BEST friends.

Lizzie had run after Isadora in the playground,

"I've lost the invitation to your party, Isadora, one of my brother's must have torn it up!" The effort and cold air brought on a coughing fit, she spat out the phlegm and wiped her nose and mouth on her sleeve.

Isadora looked at the ground.

"You can't have lost it Lizzie. I didn't send you one, my mother wouldn't let me. I wanted you to be there, I really did but my mother said I could only invite three girls and it had to be Maisie, Josie and Daisy"

"But I'm your best friend, you said so! "Tears welled up in her eyes.

Isadora took her hand and said gently;

"You are my best friend Lizzie, I begged Mum to let you come but she doesn't want you in the house, she thinks you have the illness!"

"It's just a bad cough! I always have a cold in the Winter! Mam says she's going to get me some medicine!" Lizzie wailed.

"My Mum thinks it's bad, really bad. It's CONSUMPTION!"

The word dropped into the air and seemed to hang there.

"It's not! It's not! I'm clean! I'm clean!" Lizzie's voice became a scream as everyone turned to stare at the two girls.

"My Mum worries that I'll catch something from you, just like my little brother did! I'll save you some cake!"

"Stuff your cake!" Lizzie was beside herself with anger and hurt, deep, deep hurt.

With tears pouring down her face, Lizzie ran off until her lungs felt ready to burst. She threw herself on the hard ground and cried till she could cry no more. Gulping air into her painful lungs, Lizzie sat up and there and then decided this was not going to be her life. There must be something better than this awful feeling of desperation and frustration. She made herself a promise, this would not happen to her again. Whatever it took, she would never go through this kind of humiliation again. She deserved a better life.

Watching from behind the lamppost as the lights in the house came on, the party was in full swing. Eventually, the door opened, and the girls came out, each offering their thanks for a lovely time. Lizzie began to feel strange, giddy she stumbled home, frozen to the bone. One of her little brothers was screeching, her mother was saying something over and over, but Lizzie couldn't make sense of it. Then everything went black.

Years later, Lizzie could still vividly conjure up the feeling of humiliation. She had spent the rest of the Winter in a kind of hospital and then was taken into the Care System. The rest of the family must have been as well, she never found out what happened to any of them.

However, her luck changed when she was fostered by a lady called Mrs. Green, who encouraged her to get some secretarial qualifications at night school. Mrs. Green's house was full of waifs and strays, different ones coming and going from the courts, but she still had time for each one of them. She also had some beautiful things in her house, a cabinet full of treasures and she taught Lizzie how you could tell the make of each piece and its value. Lizzie lapped up all the information like a sponge.

It was then that Lizzie started her collection. First, Mrs. Green gave her a lovely little vase. Lizzie put it on her bedside table so she could see it first thing in the morning. Soon, bit by bit, she added to it until she needed a little cupboard of her own!

Life was good, she had a job at the Electricity Board, a comfortable home with Mrs. Green, food in her stomach and then she met Frank! Tall, handsome, with a charming Irish lilt and best of all madly in love with her. She watched carefully to see how much he drank, how much money he spent, his attitude towards women his work ethic.

Her brain made notes and calculations. His prospects at the Motor factory seemed good, he was well thought of, and Mrs. Green gave her approval. Marriage was a lifetime investment and Lizzie didn't want a repeat of her own upbringing.

The years passed, Lizzie and Frank married, and bought their first little house. Two beautiful daughters followed, and Lizzie had a China cabinet with some very nice pieces, each one with their own story. Frank was made a supervisor and the family moved upwards and onwards. Each time one of their daughters had a birthday party every child in their class was invited, Lizzie made sure of that! No one was left out!

She and Frank were great neighbours, couldn't do enough for anyone and everyone. Women went to her for advice, help or a good chat. Her home was run like clockwork, her daughters were well mannered. Lizzie. Frank and the girls were a model family. The girls did well at school, one training as a nurse the other as an accountant.

When old Sarah across the road fell ill, Lizzie found time to shop for her and tend to her every need, Frank cut her grass and the girls helped when they could. The rest of the neighbours left them to it, didn't have the time!

When Sarah passed on, some of her relatives complained that items of value were missing, but how could they have known when they never visited the old girl? Some nosey parker remarked that Lizzie had a new China cabinet delivered, but really, everybody was too concerned with themselves to be bothered.

It was typical of Lizzie that when Alice down the road had a bad fall she and Frank looked after her and her house. They really set a standard that others couldn't keep up with. People meant to call in, meant to help out but with Lizzie and Frank doing it all, there was no urgency until they forgot all about Alice. Her own family were nowhere to be seen.

After Alice passed on and her house was put up for sale, one of her relatives tried to get the will changed but what did they ever do for the old girl? One of the neighbours made a nasty remark about vultures and old people being prey to them but no one remembered them ever helping anybody. Most people were just glad that Lizzie and Frank were around at the time of crisis.

The new owner of Alice's house was a widow and her daughter, who had been injured in a car crash and was in a wheelchair! Everyone felt sorry for them, but it was only Lizzie and Frank, as usual, who bothered to pop in and make them feel welcome. With holidays and family celebrations the rest of the road never got round to doing anything to help out. No one took much notice till the ambulances arrived and the news went round that sadly both the mother and daughter had suffered carbon monoxide poisoning! What a tragedy! It seems it came from some sort of heater. Neither of them survived! No one even knew their names till the details appeared on the news. Isadora and Florentina Quirke! A rumour went round that a dog walker had seen an old heater outside Lizzie and Frank's garage but nobody else saw anything and anyway, no one wanted to get involved!

To be honest no one really cared! They were just worried that the price of their properties might be affected. But hopes were raised when Lizzie and Frank put their house on the market, and it sold quickly at a great price. Mind you, it was a little palace full of antiques and China cabinets.

Life went on, Frank had been promoted to a managerial job in the Northern branch of the Motor Factory, an important step up the ladder. Everyone was sorry to see them go and meant to organize a farewell party, but no surprise, it never happened!

It was rumoured that Lizzie and her daughters had taken over a Nursing home, as one was a fully qualified nurse, the other an accountant and of course Lizzie was so good with old people, wasn't she? They couldn't be in better hands than Lizzie's, could they?

Martha's Day Out

Martha had always hated that story in the Bible, the one where Jesus rebukes one sister for wanting the other one to do her share of helping with household chores when tending to Him and his disciples!

I bet Mary was pretty, just like my sister, sitting about gazing at Jesus and looking like she understood every word He said, she thought, and Martha was a big lump like her, handy round the kitchen, her big hands kneading the bread and carrying the water to wash their feet!

Nature could be so cruel. How could two sisters be so different in looks, no wonder their mother had named one Mary and the other Martha. There was no other way to describe Mary than to say she was beautiful; she was like a China doll or a young blonde Elizabeth Taylor! Seven years older than her, Mary had enjoyed the experience of having a father around till Martha came along and frightened him off with her big shovel hands, enormous feet, hair like wire and a face only a mother could love.

The problem was she didn't believe that her mother did love her! Possibly she blamed her for the dad leaving, certainly Martha blamed her mother for him running off. People said he was a very good-looking chap with a great deal of charm.

Apparently, as the story goes, he ran off to work on the estate of a Lord and got a bit over friendly with her ladyship, producing a son but not an heir! All very Lady Chatterley and far-fetched considering he was a poorly educated lad from the East End of London. It all sounded like nonsense to her.

The annoying thing about Mary was that she was a kind and caring big sister. You couldn't help but love her!

However, Martha was the clever one at school, she had the top marks for her borough in the test for a place at the Girls Grammar School. As she was a free breakfast pupil, the borough gave an allowance for her school uniform. Martha began to thrive!

Education was her ticket out of poverty, AND she found a husband at the teacher training college! Many men trained as teachers after the Second World War and that's where she met Bernie. His skill was woodwork, and he was a member of the young Socialist club, as was she, which proved to be an excellent place for matchmaking. Bernie was a dedicated Socialist, a Labour Party man through and through, especially after his experiences during the War. He had fire in his belly, and he was going to help make a new England fit for all those who had fought and died for it!

You definitely couldn't call him handsome, but he had something about him that Martha found appealing and importantly he wouldn't be catching the eye of other women!

Soon Martha and Bernie set up home not very far from where she lived. It was a bit of a strange set up! His father was dead, and his mother was a long-term patient in a large Victorian mental hospital. Bernie and his brother Stan had been left the family home, a three-story villa. It was agreed, as Bernie was bringing his wife to the house, they would have the bottom two floors and Stan the top floor.

Not many young couples had the luxury of starting off married life in a home with no rent to pay, especially after so many houses had been bombed out of existence. Life was good for Martha, a job teaching at a local primary school and Bernie in full employment at another local secondary!

Along came a girl and then a boy, then a car and a caravan to complete the family.

Bernie got very involved with the local Labour party, distributing leaflets, knocking on doors, being on committees. He was a real firebrand!

Martha totally supported his extra curricula work and once the children were at secondary school, she applied for and got a prestigious job at a nearby Special School for girls. Her role was as a pastoral teacher, a new initiative in the Borough. Part of her remit was to run a Youth Club one evening a week.

Buzzing with ideas she planned to twin the Youth Club with a Boys Special School. This was a very controversial idea as certain people on the School Board worried about the girls and boys getting TOO friendly. However, it was a great success with games in the local park and trips to the swimming baths plus coach rides to the seaside.

Bernie and their daughter got involved which made it a real family event. Life was good.

But it was around this time that Martha felt the urge to seek out her father. Part of this was that she wanted to show him what a success she had made of her life, a life he might want to be part of? Be a grandad to her children?

Mary, her sister, had married her boss and was living a very different life in the home Counties. They had a large house with gardens that went on forever and a son at public school. To Martha their life consisted of playing golf, dining out and having cocktail parties. Having visited a very few times, Martha felt totally out of place as did Bernie who drank too much and argued politics with anyone and everyone.

This time she made an appointment to visit Mary to find out if she knew anything about their father. Amazingly, she did! She knew he had had another family and where he lived, she even had an address! Using her husband's contacts Mary had been able to trace the Lady of the Manor and found out that the illicit love story was true!

Apparently, the Lady had remained with her husband, the condition being that the child disappeared. Their father had moved on, and now was playing happy families with a new brood.

With all this information, Martha couldn't wait to get in touch even though Mary warned her that she might not be welcomed, even possibly rejected.

If she was being honest with herself, the meeting with her father wasn't everything she hoped for. Yes, he was friendly enough, certainly very handsome, but he didn't really take an interest in her achievements, only bragging about his new children who, it has to be said, stared at Martha as if she was an alien. There was no bonding whatsoever, no interest in keeping up a relationship. Truthfully, he was not what he had dreamt about over the years. He certainly never apologized for abandoning them.

Her daughter berated her:

"Mum, he left you when you were a vulnerable baby. He didn't care if you starved. He didn't care what happened to you or your sister, yet he rabbited on about his lovely new family and how much time and effort he spends with them. Doesn't that make you furious? It makes me really sad, look what our dad does for us? We don't want him as a grandad, we don't trust him?"

Her sister Mary was not sympathetic either.

"IF he had cared about us he would have been in touch, we lived in the same house for years. And don't you go blaming mum for him leaving. Do you realize she worked at a laundry during the day and cleaned railway carriages at night to keep a roof over our heads and food in our stomachs. I minded you while she was at work!"

Martha concentrated her energies on her own family and job for the next few years.

Her daughter moved in with her boyfriend and her son had a steady job where he met a very nice girl to marry.

Mary's son flourished, going to university, becoming a barrister and to Bernie's horror a Conservative MP at Westminster! And a high profile one at that! Possibly a future leader of the party! He had inherited their father's good looks and charm.

Sadly, for Bernie, New Labour came in and cleared out all the old guard, replacing them with young fresh-faced yuppies. Poor old Bernie became a casualty of the changes and got elbowed out. His wasn't the image they were after.

It wasn't all bad though. By this time, they were both retired but on good pensions. Bernie started learning to cook exotic dishes using herbs grown in the garden, they entertained friends and went to the theatre. Now they had the freedom to go on holiday anytime and anywhere they wanted to.

Probably due to his high profile, Mary's son was contacted by their missing brother, the product of his liaison with the Lady of the Manor!

Mary and Martha were cautious about meeting him, but curiosity got the better of them and a date and meeting place were arranged.

Amazingly, he was the spitting image of their father only taller and more distinguished looking, with a very cultured accent. Sadly, as part of the deal with her husband, his mother had to promise that she would never see him or try to get in touch. She kept her side of the bargain! His fate was decided. A twice removed cousin was paid to bring him up miles away from the family seat.

Needless to say, he never saw or heard from his biological father; this was also part of the deal. It was only when his guardian died that he found out what his roots were. Now at least he had two half-sisters!

Sadly, Bernie's heart gave out one afternoon while he was working in the garden.

Martha went through the various stages of bereavement until she got to Anger!

She was suddenly angry with Bernie, so she made a list of all the things his left-wing views had denied her!

When she was a child, she loved going to the local Mission Hall for Sunday School. Bernie didn't believe in God so not only was Church off the menu, but he also wouldn't even let her watch Songs of Praise on television without making fun of the sincere people taking part!

Right, she would try out the church across the road and see if it suited her!

Next, he had never allowed her to shop in the likes of Harrods or go to any of the expensive London Hotels.

Right! She phoned her sister, Mary, and arranged a day out!

First, they would go to Harrods and buy a really expensive coat, something she had secretly longed to do! Something in pure cashmere!

Next! They would have tea at the Ritz wearing this coat and share the experience with their newly found brother!

It was everything she had hoped for, the three siblings revelled in the luxurious surroundings. The food was delicious, they toasted each other in Champagne and relished the fact that they had each other. This was the life! They must do it again!

When Martha came home, she looked at the photo above the fireplace of herself and Bernie. All anger spent, she let the tears flow. She knew he would have loved her new coat and complimented her on how well the colour suited her. He would have warmly welcomed her brother as his own and found common interests with him. She had been so lucky, Bernie was not only a good husband and a wonderful father, he was a decent man, but most importantly he loved her, and she loved him.

"Mind you, Bernie", she said. I will attend a Church and although my earthy father may not have been there for me, I hope I will have a relationship with a heavenly father just like Martha and Mary in the Bible story."

And you know what, readers, she did!

I know because she was a very good friend of mine, and this story is true!

It's a Funny Old Life

If I say it myself, there is nothing to compare with a really, truthful reading from a Bonafide Medium and that's exactly what happened today. Zara is always my favourite, I feel she sees my aura really clearly, she definitely has the gift of second sight. Look, she knew straight away that I was a Libra! Ron, my husband, scoffed when I told him that.

"She saw the sign on your necklace, silly moo!" he mocked.

He's always been a sceptic; it's a cross I have to bear, but I know from years of experience whether someone is genuine or not. I mean I learned from my grandmother and my mother how to read tea leaves and look for signs, it's always been our way of life for generations. Ron says we must be descendants of gypsies: more than likely, there's plenty of those in the East End of London: no shame in that!

Anyway, back to Zara's reading! The next part was eye opening.

"You are at a crossroads in your life and soon you will meet an important person who will bring the wind of change and romance into your marriage. He comes from afar!" Spooky or what? I was able to record her deep, sensitive words and listened to it again and again. No time scale was given, to be honest there never is!

Astrology has always been my passion and throughout the ups and downs of twenty years of marriage and motherhood I have had one or two readings to help with problems. Well let's face it, life with Ron has not been a picnic though to be fair to him he is a terrific provider. His family have been car dealers for years and we live in one of the most expensive areas of Essex. I mean, we live next door to that famous footballer, you know, the one who missed the penalty at the World Cup. Lovely fellow, always ready for a chat, plays a lot of golf, happily living with a reality star.

Further down is a world champion boxer, gorgeous body on him, just a shame that he goes gaga from time to time, too many blows to the head. The rest of the year he would do anything for his neighbourhood: raising money, running Marathons then does a spell in a clinic.

Ron fits into the area really well, six foot two, completely bald, lots of tattoos which tell the story of his life, very tasteful, as is his jewellery. Boy, does he love his cars, the flashier the better. That's what first attracted me to him: I worked as a secretary for his dad and at a party someone brought out a Ouija board which kept spelling out the word METAL, or maybe it was Mental! Can't really remember.

When we met, he used to call me Twiggy; not that I am as old as her, just because I was really slim. That changed when I had my little girl, Lindy Loo. What an awful birth that was! I had to have a caesarean; they left me with a scar, right across my stomach. It was all so awful, but she was worth it, every yell, swear and scream!

Since then, there are so many things I cannot do; push a hoover round drive a car or share a bedroom with Ron. Well, his snoring wakened the baby and to be honest I didn't want to run the risk of another pregnancy; it had done so much damage to my figure, never mind my insides. Ron complained about it for a while, but he's got used to it by now. He's got a beautiful daughter, shows he's a real man and he adores her; his little princess.

A few weeks later, Zara's words came back to me, when I met the wonderful, exotic, Roberto at a spiritualist meeting at a nearby hotel. Ron was with me, grudgingly, as I needed a lift there and back. Anyway, it suited him as he wanted to give his new Roller a run. I've got to be truthful; I had made a special effort that night, my latest fur coat, only worn in safe environments, new diamond and sapphire necklace and my hair freshly styled. I felt a million dollars getting out of the shiny silver Rolls with Ron on my arm.

Roberto was from South America, via the USA. He was the most beautiful man I have ever seen in the flesh, almost pretty! So petite, dark South American colouring, really he was so good-looking it wasn't true! What a marvellous evening we had; what an amazing show he put on. Even Ron was enthralled and when we started chatting later, to our delight, Roberto jumped at the chance to come back to our house for some drinks. I could see he couldn't take his eyes off us and loved the idea of being in a real Rolls Royce. Ron was so flattered!

He certainly loved our home, it's so beautiful. I must admit that I pinched a few ideas when we visited Graceland's, the home of Elvis Presley. What classy décor! So lucky I found an interior decorator who had the same tastes. Roberto made himself right at home and hinted that he would be happy to stay with us on his next trip to England. Apparently, he prefers to be in a family setting rather than a lonely hotel room. He loves British culture!

When I blurted out about my upcoming Hysterectomy, he immediately offered to be my healer to help with renewal and go with me to the private clinic. It was all arranged there and then. You could tell that Ron really took to Roberto and it was his idea that he cleared up any other business and move in with us.

All the time I was at the Clinic, Roberto was at my side. These places are used to healers coming with the patients, so it was no problem. Mind you while I was there an Arab prince had quite a few female healers. A famous actor arrived; all very hush, hush and a vicar or priest spent a lot of time with him.

Roberto was a great comfort, and I came through my operation with flying colours. Mr. What's it, the surgeon reckoned he'd never seen scar tissue heal so fast. All in all, it was a great success and Ron was delighted, calling Roberto "OUR little

Friend". "Why don't you play with our little friend while Ron goes and makes some more money" he joked.

I loved having him around and showing him off to my friends, he was so interesting. When he spoke to you, he looked right into your eyes as if he could see your very soul. Only one of my friends was not sure of his intentions, and he didn't seem to like her, in fact warned me to keep my distance from her. My head was so far in the clouds with his constant attention and healing that I didn't listen to her doubts even though she had been a friend for years.

Sometimes Ron would take him UP West to see other clients and they would be gone all day. Still, I didn't have exclusive rights to his healing powers, the rest of the world needed him.

It was around this time that our daughter, Lindy Loo started to play up, I caught her trying to kick Roberto and she kept asking when he was leaving! She seemed to be clingy especially to her dad. Just jealous, I thought. Attention seeking!

When I look back to that time, I realize that I missed all the signs. Should have had another reading from Zara or someone else. The funny thing is you can have all the Astronomical information in the world and not see what is under your own nose. Too much smoke and mirrors instead of common sense.

Strange how it all turned out, not quite what I thought Zara meant when she gave me the reading, mentioning being at a crossroads and romance in my marriage. I thought she meant me!! Honestly, you never really know somebody, well only if you are paying attention, which I wasn't.

At least they are happy together, Ron and Roberto, or Roberta, as she calls herself now. Seems she had the "OP" at my Clinic; found all about it when he/she was there helping me. They make a good-looking pair, in fairness and have moved to America. Great cars there, Ron!

I can't complain, I moved in with the footballer next door when his reality star girlfriend ran off with her partner on a dancing show. He never misses a penalty with me!! If you know what I mean. And Lindy Loo? She got over her jealousy of Roberto and spends half the year with them.

I wonder what the future holds for us all? Maybe I'll make an appointment with Zara! It's a funny old life, isn't it?

Happy Birthday Dusty

It was the morning of my forty-second birthday that I realized I did not love my husband; in fact, I realized that I had never loved him!

Watching him wander about our bedroom in his psychedelic y-fronts awakened in me a feeling of revulsion.

As my eyes followed him, I was astounded that I, a person of sound mind, had spent the last fifteen years married to someone as appalling as Des. Where was the dream lover of my adolescent years? Des couldn't arouse enough passion in me to shift sand in an egg timer!

What was he droning on about and why was he wearing out our already threadbare carpet this early on a Saturday morning? And it was my birthday! Not that anyone cared!

Now he was off to the bathroom with our portable radio, tuned to a Sixties music channel.

Where were the chocolates, flowers, breakfast in bed?

Suddenly an awful thought entered my head! I am forty-two! Elvis was forty-two when he died! It's time I started doing something for myself, just for me, before it is TOO late!

"Mum, can you tell Dad to turn off that horrible racket, some of us are trying to get some sleep!"

A door slammed shut: the sounds of Dusty Springfield grew louder and louder.

Coming back to the bedroom he threw a small package at me.

"Happy birthday, Dusty!"

By the way, he calls me Dusty sometimes as she and I have the same birthday 16th April, but not the same year! It's 1987 and she must be nearly fifty!

"You thought I'd forgotten, didn't you?"

The package was wrapped in a serviette from the Taj Mahal Restaurant and the aroma was pure Madras!

Well, well, it was a pair of black crotchless panties with ROOM FOR A BIG ONE printed delicately in mauve!

"This bloke was flogging them in the Dog and Ferrett last night. As soon as I saw them, I thought old Dusty would love these. She likes novelties."

How true! I do love novelties, specially anything to do with sex. Anything remotely to do with sex is a novelty in our marriage!

Des was now wearing his supporter's outfit. Of course, that's why he is up so early, he is off to London with his football club. The coach will be leaving soon. Des

never misses a match, not even on my birthday.

Not even when the kids were born!

Loyalty to the club comes first every time!

I had a brain wave! If he was going to London, maybe I should go as well! There must be room on the coach for the club secretary's wife!

Strangely, Des wasn't too keen. Yes, there was room on the coach but no ticket for the game. Well, that didn't matter, I had no intention to go all the way to London to be bored to death!

It was MY birthday, and I was going to grab life by the throat even if it meant hijacking a football coach!

Getting dressed in a fabulous new outfit I had bought at the Precinct and pulling a comb through my hair, there was no time to do make-up; that could be done during one of the stops on the way, I planned out my day.

Now, I love visiting posh hotels: it's what I like to do when I have the time. It's my Secret Pleasure!

Just for fun, I put on the crotchless panties to see if they made me feel any different. The new me needed a fresh image, maybe a naughty one!

Now, Andy is Des' best mate, more than that he is Des' mentor ever since he advised him in the school playground on marble swaps. In another civilization, Andy would be the village wise man, a thrower of bones, a joint owner of pigeons, a Know all!

They always sit together on the coach, so who was I to come between such a beautiful friendship?

I took my place on a seat over the wheels, where else? An icy breeze wafted over me emanating from the cold shoulders I was being given.

"Wives coming on the coach, Whatever next?"

Someone joked,

"I'll tell you what's next! They'll want to play on the team!"

Roars of laughter, well this was 1987!

At least on this journey I would have the pleasure of my own company. I could beautify myself in the Ladies during the stops and nod off if there was community singing. Oddly enough, my presence seemed to have put a damper on the choice of musical material!

On reaching London, I said my fond farewell to Des and arranged where and when to meet up for the return journey.

Now my adventure was about to begin!

Browsing round a large department store I noticed a sales promotion for Erotica, a new perfume enticingly advertised as "Find the real you" That sounded exactly what I needed to do! The price was ridiculously high, but it included in the purchase, for one day only, a complete facial makeover suited to one's own personality. Why not, I thought, it's your birthday, go for it!

There is nothing more relaxing than being pampered. The young lady said she knew what my personality was and set about creating it.

When she had finished and I had been sprayed extensively with Erotica, I paid for my very small bottle and looked into the mirror she offered.

Well! It was colourful, no doubt about that!

I set off for the nearest, most posh hotel I could find.

Now, I have always found that more expensive hotels cater very well for women on their own especially if they look like they have a bob or two. You really need a bit of swagger and self-assurance. With my new look I was full of confidence.

The staff were charming, and I was welcomed into the gorgeous bar area which smelt nearly as good as I did.

Feeling quite hungry, by now, I ordered my favourite smoked salmon sandwiches and a Pimm's Number One, suitably sophisticated!

Soon I was feeling a warm glow, totally relaxed: I can recommend this experience for any jaded, put upon wife and mother.

The bar area was pleasantly busy, certainly enough to make it interesting, I was ready to order another drink when I heard a voice,

"May I join you?"

Good God, it was him off the tele, one of Des' favourite probing, left wing interviewers! He looked a lot more handsome and groomed in real life with well cut, expensive clothes.

"I think we have met before, at a BBC function last Christmas."

Well, if he wanted to make up a lie, who was I to correct him?

It's funny with people who are regularly on television, you feel as if you know them and that they know you! I didn't know they felt the same way?

He was so charming, and his voice was much more cultured that how he sounded on those political programmes where he grilled anyone and everyone with "A Man of the People" Northern burr!

When the waiter came over, he ordered more drinks and we chatted comfortably about this and that. He was very easy to talk to.

Apparently, he was staying at the hotel for a few days and told me about this amazing painting on the wall of his room. He wondered if it was an original could it be? By the time I had got through my third Pimm's, I was very eager to examine the painting for myself. Another one of my many gifts is a knowledge of Renaissance painters! Or maybe not!

Let's just say, some things were more real than others. The message on my panties for one!

Back on the coach, faces were glum, another defeat, two points lost, a further slide down the league table. Des was despondent, Andy was full of advice for the referee; mostly how he could rearrange his vital organs and extremely knowledgeable about the sexual predilections of the opposing team.

The return journey was a silent affair interspersed by short stops to aid the lifting of heavy hearts and the relieving of groaning bladders.

Des and I walked home together. Now the good thing about Des is that he doesn't stay miserable for long.

"Well Dusty, what would you like to do this evening? It is your birthday. How about a pub crawl ending up at the DOG and FERRETT, followed by a hot curry at the Taj Mahal? We could even try out those new panties of yours?"

Now, let's be honest. What woman could resist an offer like that?

Well! Being forty-two isn't so bad after all! There's life in the old girl yet!

I wonder where the next away match is?

Happy Birthday Dusty

EDDIE

His heart was pounding as he approached the school gates. Something funny was going on, where were the other pupils?

He had seen his teacher walk past at her usual time from the Station. Eddie often looked out for her from the balcony of the block of flats where he and his family lived.

There was no one about except the caretaker!

"No school for you today, Eddie. You're in luck! You can go back to bed," he chuckled.

"What's going on? I saw my teacher walking down the road!" He began to sweat.

"The lorry drivers who bring the fuel to heat the premises are on strike. There's no heat in the building. The teachers have to turn up. We can keep the staffroom warm with an electric fire. They will have to huddle together in there. Let's hope they like each other's company and have brought their own food as the kitchen is closed", he laughed loudly.

"But I'm not cold!" Eddie was beginning to panic.

"Rules are rules, no heat, no pupils! All the schools in London are closed, it's been all over the news. How come you didn't know?"

Eddie's Mum worked at night cleaning train carriages; Dad was on late shift. No one was awake to tell him anything.

"When will the school be open?"

"Who knows! These guys mean business! Go off and enjoy yourself, son!"

Obviously, the caretaker didn't understand how important all of this was to Eddie! This was a catastrophe! What was he going to do?

Eddie was in his last year at Primary School, so far, he had never missed a day's attendance and had a certificate for each year. If he managed to complete this school year, he would get a prize from the Education Authority and the chance to stand up in morning assembly when everyone would clap.

He had imagined it all so many times, standing on the stage with the headteacher shaking his hand and all the kids looking at him in admiration! The sound of all that applause! It would be the biggest, most important day of his life!

Now, the dream could be about to disappear! It was the only thing he was good at: attending school! The only prize he was ever going to be in with a certain chance of winning was the Attendance Prize!

Good attendance was very important in their school. The class with the best attendance every week got to have the Shield in their room, pride of place for all to see. Eddie thought it was the most beautiful thing he had ever seen!

Sadly, there was no prize for coming last, his class had the worst record in the school. Some nasty people said they were the Dunces' class. Miss used to joke, "Who's calling ME a Dunce!" But they all knew that they were!

Some of his classmates hardly ever turned up! Some never arrived till the afternoon so that didn't count either. One family had done a "Moonlight Flit" so were still on the roll but always absent! Nobody knew where they had gone and until they were on the books of another school, they were technically absent! Two of them were in his class! They just didn't stand a chance of winning the Shield!

Eddie worked really hard at school, behaved himself, was polite and tried to be helpful, that was on his school reports every year! His parents were very proud of him.

Unfortunately, he didn't get good marks in any subjects. It was all so hard! He tried and tried. He got extra help with reading, and he knew it was important that he made progress as his dream job was to work at the Ford factory in Dagenham.

Fancy being able to make all those cars! His dad's job was working there, and he had shown them pictures from a Ford's brochure. Wow! They were SO beautiful and colourful, he knew the names of them all! His dad explained that you had to be able to read the safety instructions in the huge factory before they gave you a job, even for sweeping up and cleaning.

At least he was good at counting and numbers and had been chosen and trusted as a milk monitor. Every day he and his friend John had to sort out how many milk bottles each class needed. This was a great job; Eddie felt really important going from class to class, knocking on the doors delivering the crates, plus you often got an extra bottle from the leftovers! He couldn't understand why some people pulled a face when drinking the milk. It was the only thing he had for breakfast and before his school dinner.

Oh No! Now that the school was closed, he would miss out. His mum relied on the free milk and school dinners, so she didn't have to make a meal during the week.

Also, it was their class's day for going to Canning Town Library! Eddie loved that outing. The whole class followed behind Miss in two's carrying their library book from the time before and then looked around for another one to replace it when they got there. The library was a very posh building with lots of stairs. You had to be really quiet inside, no running or mucking about.

Eddie and his partner John always tried to find the biggest books so that they could show off on the way back. It was great if the kids from Star Lane School were out playing in the playground. Fortunately, they were safely behind the fence as they always yelled at them. That was fun! Miss always said to ignore them, but Eddie and John made sure to show off the size of their books! Both boys kept the library books in their desk for safekeeping. No point in taking risks. They were scared of losing them and not being able to go back!

Eddie would never even think of going to Canning Town Library on his own, even though the lady there said they could. He was sure they wouldn't let the likes of him in on his own.

What was he going to do! He thought hard, yes, he could spend the day at the Adventure Playground except it didn't open till after school! Perhaps John might be about, and they could chase each other round the park. But how was he going to find out when the school would reopen?

The only solution was to turn up at school every morning and check!

And that is exactly what Eddie did! Every morning there he was at the school gates, well on time, until that happy day when the strike was called off, the oil and food flowed into the school premises and normality was restored.

By the end of the school year, he had not missed a single day and at the final assembly Eddie was invited up onto the stage to claim his prize, which was a book and a suitably big book plus the most wonderful certificate with his name written in gold letters! The head teacher shook his hand and said that the whole school was proud of such an achievement!

He was the only pupil in the school's records to have completed four years with full attendance! What a claim to fame! Eddie stood there looking at all the smiling faces of pupils and staff and listening to all that glorious applause!

This was something to be proud of, something he would never forget, and little did he know it was something his teacher would write about Fifty years later!

....
....

A Postscript.

During that strike I went with another teacher called Margaret to visit a school in East Ham. We had very little to do with no pupils to teach so it made a nice break. At the school I met a young Irish girl called Sue and we became instant friends. She was from Dublin and had some relatives in my hometown.

Later, the Council flats which Eddie lived in were gentrified with the coming of the Jubilee Line. Amazingly, Sue and her husband lived for a while in these very Buildings, and I visited them there on the way to my Headteacher's retirement party.

Sue and I remained friends for the next thirty years until her sudden death from a brain Haemorrhage. If it had not been for the tanker drivers' strike, we may have never met! Serendipity or what!

REMINISCENCES

Friends

"Go back and live with your English Queen, you don't belong here, you're not Irish, you're English!"

"What are you talking about? Of course, I'm Irish, I was born here as were my family going back generations!"

"No, you're not, you come from the Black North, your lot are all English! Go and live with your English Queen. You should leave Ireland to the Irish!"

I looked at her face, was she being silly, joking around? She couldn't be serious, could she? Never in my life had anyone said that to me. Yes, I had been shouted at on the way home from school;

"Protestant Dick went up the stick and never came down till Monday Wick"

Don't ask me what that means or meant, haven't a clue, but it was frequently accompanied by stones hurled after my sister and I if we took a chance running across a railway bridge, as a short cut home from Primary school. It was probably quite fortuitous that we didn't have a clue what to shout back! Yes, I knew we were a divided community in our town, you had to be careful who you mixed with, but no one ever said we weren't Irish. We knew we were!

However, this was a very different situation. The girl who was telling me I wasn't Irish was supposedly a friend! We were sitting in her family home in Limerick in the Republic of Ireland: I was an invited guest.

How had I ended up so far from my home in the" Black" North; staying with a family who HAD regarded me as one of THEM when we were working in England, but really viewed me as an interloper? Not a nice feeling! To me it didn't make sense! Being only sixteen years of age, I had never been in the South of Ireland before, and these were the first "Irish" Republicans I had ever met.

"Stop teasing the child!" their mother rebuked Siobhan, one of the sisters.

"She can't help where she comes from!"

I think that was the exact moment my trust in people died. From then on, I never, ever, let my guard down or took anything anyone said at face value. You always need to protect yourself.

Along with my red hair, pale skin which refused to tan, only burn, freckles everywhere, I looked typically Irish! Didn't I?

Siobhan was one of four sisters who had befriended me in Great Yarmouth several weeks ago. Mammy arranged that my own sisters, who had worked there the previous year, get me a job working for an Italian family who owned a string of cafes. It had all sounded a great way of making some money and spending the summer holidays at the seaside.

Arrangements were made, a friend of my oldest sister would accompany me as she was going there to work. Jennifer and I flew off to London, stopped by to spend the afternoon with her aunt, and caught the train to Great Yarmouth. So far so good! Jennifer was at least seven years older than me, thus very sensible and I felt quite safe as she knew her way around. Or so I hoped!

However, when we reached the address, we had been given, in Regent Road, I discovered that my oldest sister had moved on to pastures new and my other sister wasn't due to arrive till later in the month. There I was at sixteen on my own, stranded in another country, surrounded by strangers, and had never worked before. Well at least I had Jennifer!

The evening found me settled in a dormitory of bunk beds above a café. I was going to be part of a team that opened up the newest café, the BIG V, which was just across the road. We could eat at any of the family's cafes and chip shops. Sounded fine. Bunk beds were new to me but Heigh! Ho! I was exhausted and would have fallen asleep anywhere.

Next day found our merry band of girls learning how to use and maintain an ice cream machine, make a variety of ice cream sundaes, flip burgers with onions, fry eggs and bacon and use the new expensive coffee machine. Few of us were allowed to use this impressive piece of Italian equipment, I wasn't old enough, but Jennifer was.

Sadly, two days later, the brand-new coffee machine expelled so much pressurized steam that it exploded all over Jennifer's face! She was scalded and carted off to hospital. Oh no! Poor girl! In Hospital and possibly scarred so far away from home.

However, thankfully, it wasn't as bad as it looked: the first aid she had been given worked well but she decided to go and recover at her aunt's house in London. A sensible move but one which left me all alone in a strange land! I would just have to cope!

A lot of the training was about cleaning, learning the tricks of the trade, especially using the till: giving change, checking whether you had been given a pound note or a five note. This was vitally important as the till was checked every night.

My specialty, I am proud to say, was how to take the cold milk machine apart for cleaning and put it together again! To be honest, I just happened to be there when the engineer was installing it!

We were warned, if anyone asked for a baby's bottle to be filled, we must only use the fresh milk from the churn. Inspectors came regularly to check weights and measures: the cold milk in the machine was watered down! What a surprise!

There were quite a few tricks of the trade in 1961!

Sandwiches which started to curl would be put to the bottom of the pile. If they fell onto the floor they were picked up and dusted down.

Chicken rolls, which we learned to make, used every bit of the chicken, nothing was thrown away! And I mean nothing! One of these became a missile one night from a very dissatisfied customer!

Frothy coffee and Horlicks were made in big jugs during busy times. There were two shows a night and the holidaymakers poured out of the theatres in their droves ready for refreshments.

Cold drinks were served BEFORE cups of tea as the turnover was bigger.

The biggest con of all was that although the family were Italian, they had on the menu, Spaghetti products which were out of tins!

I remember being asked if the spaghetti was authentically Italian! Knowing full well it came out of a tin, I referred them to one of the family. Another dissatisfied customer!

However, the burgers, bacon rolls and especially the ice cream, which was genuinely Italian, were delicious. So, as long as the sun shone, and the entertainment was first class, most holidaymakers were jolly and appreciative of our efforts.

So here I was, no sisters, and now no Jennifer! All alone until the Fenton family, just arrived from the South of Ireland, took me under their collective wings. Out of the four of them, Theresa was my age, the others were older. Theresa and I shared a bunk bed and worked at the same café. We hit it off straight away, she had a great sense of fun. Her sisters all seemed nice girls though I didn't see much of them as they worked in different cafes around Regent Road.

My spirits were lifted especially as I found the work in the café quite easy. Now I had good company as well as someone to spend my free time with. Theresa and I enjoyed the same kind of music, films, food. Our main boss was the owner and father of several daughters. Each one had a cafe to look after and we had struck lucky with the youngest and sweetest, Louisa!

One evening Teresa and I set off to see one of the many shows in town with her sister Siobhan. Siobhan really liked a particular pop singer who had recently won the top spot in the charts. After it finished, she wanted to go round to the stage door to meet him. Fluttering her eyelashes and turning on all of her Irish charm, she soon was having an exclusive chat about their joint love of horse riding.

The upshot was a date arranged for the next morning! Now I found this shocking as the afternoon before, I had served the same guy, his WIFE and child in our café.! They had seemed like a lovely couple and now he was going on a date with Siobhan, who also had a steady boyfriend back home! Shocking or what! You couldn't make it up!

As it turned out, this had long ranging outcomes. Siobhan went off on her date, missed going to work, the boss found out what she had been up to, as she had been bragging to anyone who would listen. Guess what? She got the sack!

Now when you live in, getting the sack is a serious business!

The next thing the sisters came to see me and said that they were ALL leaving and returning to Ireland!

In a panic and scared of being left on my own I agreed that, if the boss would let me, I would leave with them!

As it was near the end of the season, he was only too glad to see the back of us. Wages were paid up, flights booked and the next thing I knew I was ringing my parents from Shannon Airport in Limerick to let them know where I was! We then travelled to a railway station and were picked up by the girls' brother and were only too glad to have a meal and go to bed; I was sharing with Teresa.

The family lived in a rambling, slightly run-down Georgian farmhouse and made their money by breeding greyhounds. It was our task to walk these beautiful creatures and they all seemed very tame and obliging.

However once off the lead was another matter. Suddenly, we heard a shout from a very irate farmer nearby. When we went over to see what he wanted, to our horror we saw three sheep lying on the ground! That's when I learned that dogs could worry sheep to death!

It all happened so quickly; it was unbelievable, especially as neither of the sisters seemed too bothered! More important was which dance they were going to attend at the weekend!

Apparently, Saturday night was for dancing, and we all got ready to travel to the nearest Dance Hall. Nothing I liked better! Roger, their brother drove some of us, Siobhan's boyfriend followed on with the rest. So, all in all, we made quite an entrance to a dimly lit Hall in the middle of nowhere.

It was obvious that the girls at the dance, who were keeping an eye on the door for talent, were extremely disappointed to see so many girls and so few men arrive!

Worse was to come when the handsome Roger decided he wanted to dance most of the night with me, a total stranger! I could feel the daggers in my back!

These country dances started late and ended in the early hours of the morning! But no matter how tired, Mass was a must on the Sunday morning.

Now, after Siobhan's comments, I had made it clear that I wanted to go to a Protestant church on Sunday: I would not be joining them at Mass.

This caused a stir, for according to them, when people attended the Protestant church, they had to fall in front of and worship a large eagle. Failure to adhere to this would cause a shift in the floor, a large expanse of water would appear, the offender thrown into it, fully clothed and held down until they confessed their sins!

How did they know all this, never having been in the church? Well, the woman who cleaned the building swore it was true! So, it must be!

Fully warned, I was brave enough to insist that they deliver me to the door, I would take my chances!

"If I come out dripping wet, you will know why!"

The most exciting experience I had at this very small church was that the vicar was also the organist, so when he announced a hymn, he had to come down from the pulpit and warm up the organ pipes. I had never seen so few people attend a service!

The family were delighted to find me safe and dry when they came to pick me up. By the way, there was an eagle, it was the Bible rest! No sign of any water, even the font was empty!

Siobhan's boyfriend kindly offered to show me some of the local beauty spots, which was lovely of him.

I think he was part saint for putting up with Siobhan. Every time, in her opinion, he went too fast or didn't stop when she wanted him to, she threatened to throw herself out of the car! What was she like? Actually, she was the biggest pain ever, completely full of herself and so unlike the other sisters who were really nice.

Eventually, she frightened the life out of us when she really did open the car door while we were moving! What she hoped the outcome would be if she fell out, was anybody's guess!

Most of the sisters, except for Teresa, were students at University College in Dublin, she was at Art College, so they had a flat nearby.

The next move was to drive up to Dublin and stay for a few days. It was going to be pure gas!

It was 1961 and that part of Dublin was really run down. I had never seen anything like it, quite shocking! The small flat was in a permanent state of disarray, I slept on the floor. We went out dancing every night and slept late into the day.

Suddenly, one morning someone came in and started shouting at us. Startled, I soon became aware that it was yet another sister who was not amused at the squalor we were living in!

It turned out that she was the sensible one! A medical student, she set about giving us very clear directions on how to tidy HER flat up! She really cracked the whip! A scary lady!

It was time for me to head home. The sisters accompanied me to the railway station and in their usual mad way, insisted on getting me a child's ticket!

"Sure, why would you spend all that money when you don't need to? You can easily pass for twelve!"

Holding my breath, I offered my ticket to the very cross-looking collector, while my friends waited to wave me goodbye.

Looking me up and down he said, sarcastically,

"Mind yourself crossing the road, child!"

When you are young you are used to adults telling you off, so as long as I got on the train, it was just "pure fecking gas". An expression I had learned from my Irish friends!

Mind you, there were still the border guards to face. In those days, they came on board and searched every bag you had. No problem for me as I wasn't smuggling anything other than dirty washing!

My parents were relieved to see me, and I was ready to sleep for a week.

Teresa had told me that some people in the greyhound racing world were full of superstitions. One man they knew would turn back on his way to a race if he saw a redheaded woman.

Well just after this redhead had left, their best greyhound dropped dead! Coincidence or hocus-pocus! Perhaps Siobhan shouldn't have insulted me! We Northerners have our own ways of seeking revenge.

We exchanged a few letters now and again but never managed to meet up.

I got on with my education and when I qualified as a teacher, I took Siobhan's advice and went to live and work in London nice and near to my English Queen.

Summers in Great Yarmouth

Statuesque is the best word to describe Rene, probably about 5ft 10" and solidly built, with a charming smile and an English accent which wasn't familiar to my Northern Ireland ear.

"I'm Rene, my love, and I am the manageress of this café. Now I will tell you what you need to know to work here"

Here, was Alfredo's café in Great Yarmouth, Norfolk. I had worked during the previous Summer for a large rival Italian chain. Having spent some time in this café and chatted to the young twin boys whose father owned it; the idea had come that I should return this Summer and work for them! Seemed like a plan and a smack in the mouth for the other people. The boys' father relished the idea of old Big Italian guy, walking past, looking in and seeing little old me, working for them! Pretty far-fetched considering Mr. Italy had lots of establishments and hundreds of employees! Though to be fair, I had built up a friendship with his youngest daughter and one of the twins told her that I was coming to work for them.

I'm sure he was devastated!!Certainly he glared in a few times when he did his daily walk between his cafes and restaurants. Mind you all the café owners investigated each other's places to see how busy they were.

Oh, I forgot to tell you, I lived with the family above the café in Regent Road, the main street which led to the beach and piers at one end, the market and railway station at the other end.

To me, coming from a small town in Northern Ireland, Great Yarmouth was the most fabulous place, full of bright lights, theatres, advertising the biggest names in show business, restaurants, fun fairs and buzzing with holiday makers. Of course, this was 1962!

Honestly, you couldn't think of a more gainful way to spend your school holidays. Having a job, earning money and experiencing real life was a lot better than sitting about being bored and skint at home. The added benefit was that lots of students from Ireland worked in and around that area during the summer months. It's hard to believe, now, but some were employed as bus conductors, Bird's Eye factory employees and at holiday camps!

Just thinking back to those days gives me a buzz. I was seventeen. At sweet sixteen I had already spent one Summer there, sharing accommodation with lots of Irish girls, learning how to flip burgers, fill an ice cream cone from very temperamental machines, brew up frothy coffee and do calculations in my head, making sure the correct change was given. I could make Knickerbocker Glories and ice cream sundaes all day long!

Rene showed me how things were done in Alfredos, the does and don'ts, what kept the boss happy. My hours were from eight am till 6pm with the evening off, Saturday, working till closing and Sunday till 2pm. Of course, as I was conveniently upstairs, I might be needed to fill in if someone didn't turn up, which happened regularly!

The turnover of staff was huge as many workers were itinerants who went from place to place. Accommodation was always offered but this didn't stop people doing a moonlight flit. The boss was very hard to please, especially if he'd had a bad day at Yarmouth races, everyone including the customers, would be in for a taste of his violent temper!! Don't sit too long over a cup of tea or be caught writing postcards!

"This isn't the blankety, blank post office!"

Definitely don't complain that Sunday's prices were different to Mondays! Why? Who knew! Making money from day trippers, which backfired when holiday makers came from Saturday for a week and then complained that they had been overcharged over the weekend!

Rene was married and lived in Great Yarmouth, with a good track record so she was the best kind of worker. Originally, she was from Sheffield and had met her husband in the army. I had never met a woman who had served, in fact, come to think of it, I don't think I have met one since!

During her time in the army, she began a singing career with a band, and continued this in the evenings and at weekends. Composing songs was also her passion and she said that a very well-known hit song of the era was actually her work but had been stolen by another member of the band who had the right contacts and had helped her with the music! She hadn't been able to prove ownership, so lost out big time as it was one of those songs that you could retire on: permanently still on wedding play lists! Unbelievable! What a loss!

She proved a very good friend to me and was as honest as the day was long and our days were very, very long! Her aim was to cook me a meal at her house, stew with dumplings which was her specialty. So, one evening found me on the bus to New Town area of Great Yarmouth. True to her word she made me a wonderful meal with the tastiest dumplings! I spent a warm cosy evening with her and her husband, a lasting memory.

It was time for me to return home to the Emerald Isle, with my hard-earned wages safe in my hands plus a generous bonus from the Boss, a promise of returning the next year and a wrapped present from Rene.

Inside the package I found a beautiful, antique necklace with a note which said,

"A real friendship is hard to find, but we managed it, love Rene"

I kept up a correspondence with her for several years and met up when I came back to Great Yarmouth to work for two more Summers, she sent me photos of her twin daughters and son. In fact, I found these the other day when I was having a clear up. I invited her to my wedding in 1971. I would have loved to have had her there, but it was too difficult for her to travel so far and too expensive.

Looking at her kind, strong, honest face in the photographs, I get a warm glow; she was a beautiful soul. I hope the fates were kind to her: she certainly had qualities that deserved blessings. Rene was my friend.

I loved those twin boys, whose father owned the cafe; they were my little summer brothers. We had so much fun going to see shows together; we saw them all! Slipping out for meals in the Greek restaurant opposite and sneaking in again! Their father was very strict with them and with me. Keeping them company when unsavoury, sometimes well-known showbusiness people tried to hit on them. Part Italian and small, they were too cute for their own safety!

 Sadly, one has died but we were friends till the end, and I am still in touch with the other one and plan to meet up soon!

Great Yarmouth has a special place in my heart. I learned so much there which was a different, a very different kind of education.

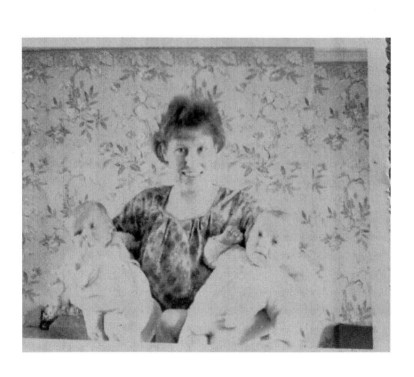

My Sixties

I always say that the Swinging Sixties began in 1966, which was the year when England won the World Cup IN England. Guess who was fortunate to be starting their teaching careers at that very time? Yes, my flat mate and little old me, straight off the boat from Northern Ireland.

Christmas was coming up and we wanted to return home in triumph, so promising each other that we would only talk about the positive aspects of our lives, we set about deciding what to wear as clothes and hairstyles showed success.

From September, when we began work, we had been paying emergency tax, so our December pay included a large, well large to us, tax back! Hurrah! Let's splash some serious cash! Straight up to the big C&A's in East Ham High Street. Where else?

I purchased a beautiful brown coat with a huge fur collar, a fawn shirt dress, the latest fashion, and a black rabbit skin snood. Later a pair of brown high heeled shoes completed the outfit. So sophisticated!

While travelling to Liverpool, as we looked so good, we decided to treat ourselves to a meal on the train. White table clothes, silver service, three courses, we took it all in our stride. Wow! This was the life!

Maybe it wasn't the wisest option: a few hours later the overnight ferry to Belfast heaved and tossed its way across the Irish Sea. Sitting in the tearoom a sailor shouted:

"If you two are going to throw up, go outside!"

Charming! Who was he talking to? There was no way we were going to spoil our new coats by boking (a Northern Irish expression for vomiting) over them!

When the boat landed and we were met by our fathers, eagerly waiting, we were the epitome of London Fashion, well we hoped we were!

Certainly, I knew the fawn shirt dress was a winner when on Christmas Day my older sister asked if I would like to swap dresses with her! Cheeky or what? Considering that she was the most stylish person I knew, and was wearing a carefully chosen outfit, I regarded this as a win!

Next my sister announced her wedding, which would be held in London: I knew I had to find something special. Now, I'm not a great believer in mysticism, fate yes, but I've got to say that I was LED to a shop window in Oxford Street where the most amazing outfit was beckoning to me! To this day I can conjure up the experience!

It fitted me perfectly; I just wish I had a photograph! Let me describe it: A tartan mini kilt, green and dark red; a tweed jacket with lapels that matched the tartan, two back splits; to set it off, a tartan cap or as we called it a touree! You know, you can fall in love with clothes, and this was a match made in heaven.

Who invented trouser suits for women? Don't know, will have to Goggle it!

I had two beauties. The first one was black and white check: this was the period of OP ART. The must-have item to set it off was a pair of leather driving gloves, they were all the rage. Mine were a gorgeous black and white pair, very snug fit, and purchased at an expensive store on Oxford Street, maybe Marshall & Snelgrove. I then added black and white earrings, and a black and white handbag. I already had black boots. My ensemble was complete! I felt fantastic, ready for anything!

Not content with one trouser suit, I went looking for another and stumbled across a purple beauty in Carnaby Street. How I loved this street! Every time I visit London I pop by and relive my youth.

The Beatles had made old army uniforms very popular, so I was delighted with my latest purchase: the jacket had a stand-up collar and there were metal buttons right up to the neck, a very military look. I don't recall how much it cost but the material was of a very high quality. I have always loved the colour purple, as it set off my red hair, and this was a lovely shade of African Violet.

It was too smart for any old occasion, so I put it safely in my wardrobe.

My sister came over from Ireland to stay with me as she had some function to attend in London. Later that evening, when my flat-mate and I had been at work all day, the doorbell rang. There standing as bold as brass was my sister, wearing my new purple trouser suit!!

"You're wearing my new suit!" I gasped. "I haven't even worn it yet!"

Without a bit of embarrassment, she shrugged,

"I looked through your wardrobe and this suit was nicer than the one I brought with me"

My flat mate and I were speechless!

The next time she came to London, perhaps as an apology, she gave me a huge sheepskin that she had purchased on her many travels. It was quite spectacular, even more so than the one Cher had worn on their first time on British T V. It could be worn skin side out or fur side out, the zip worked either way.

Further down our road lived a large old English sheepdog who regularly slept outside his home. One day, as I walked by, the dog decided to grab my furry arm, obviously thinking I was a sheep! Probably smelt like one! When I yelled out, a family member reassured me that the old fellow wouldn't hurt a fly! Well, it might very well hurt a sheep: wasn't it a sheep dog?

I had a lot of good times in that coat!

Another fashion which came and went was wearing second-hand fur coats. Sounds strange and not very politically correct nowadays, doesn't it?

Just by chance a teacher on my staff had an old aunt pass away and guess what? She had left her several fur coats! You couldn't make it up, could you? My flat mate and I hot footed it round to her house and we had first pick. After trying them on, I chose a Musquash, which was lovely and soft, and my flat mate choice was a Pony skin, both at a reasonable giveaway price! Result! Useful for those cold Winter days on playground duty.

Now sometimes I was invited to somewhere really posh and required the clothes to match. For instance, my sister's sister-in-law lived in a flat in Chelsea! Yes, you heard right! Chelsea in the Sixties and just off King's Road. Unbelievable! She had these amazing parties with guests from the literary world so when I was invited, my sister would warn me to push the boat out and dress accordingly. Well, I could be trusted not to let our side of the family down.

Probably in those golden days, my best feature was my long thick red hair. A hairdresser that I knew could do the most wonderful up to date styles and I would end up with anything that old Vidal Sassoon could conjure up on a good day!

My legs were pretty enviable as well and there were so many pretty dresses to be had: Chelsea Girl was often a winning hunting ground for me. Stiletto heels were not the most comfortable footwear, it has to be said but they made you walk with a wiggle!

My father worked for an oil company and every now and again he would be in London on business. He would always try to meet up and on one memorable occasion, my flat mate and I were invited to join him and his colleagues to a dinner at the Great Eastern Hotel at Liverpool station. As my father had been mayor of our town twice, I was used to partnering him to various functions. Therefore, he trusted me not to let the side down!! Very important in our family!

This was an important business deal for the company and a large contract was to be signed. My flat mate and I were always good company and full of youthful exuberance. That night, full of beans and dolled up in our latest dresses we entered the Great Eastern Hotel, where a variety of events were taking place. At the reception desk, a very large photo of a renowned fashion designer was on display.

"Are you girls Mary Quant models?" asked the guy at reception, pointing to the placard advertising the fashion show which was being held that very night!

Well! The question has to be asked: what would have happened if we had said "Yes, we are!" We will never know!

The next question is, how good did we look that night?

What I do know is that we went down a storm with my fathers' colleagues that, not only was a huge contract signed, but the man signing it insisted on paying for everyone's meal. My Father was delighted, we were made a great fuss of and went home full of the joys of youth.

I count myself so lucky to have been young in Sixties London. Most of all I was so fortunate to have a wonderful, compatible, compassionate, fun-loving flat mate to share all our adventures. Thank you, Jayne, you have always been my beautiful soul mate.

London

I don't know how you feel about London, but I fell under its spell at the tender age of eleven. This is what happened.

My best friend at Primary school from the age of four, in Northern Ireland, was Adrienne, she had very blonde hair, mine was red and we both wore glasses. I had read Anne of Green Gables and knew, just as Anne did about her special friend, that Adrienne and I were kindred spirits.

Adrienne had an older brother who was married and lived on the Caribbean Island of Tobago, and if you think that was exotic, well, listen to this!

HER BIG SISTER, OLIVE, WAS AN AIR HOSTESS IN LONDON! It does not get any better than that now, does it?

I never met her brother, but her sister had breezed into our classroom one day to pick Adrienne up. She was the most glamorous person I had ever seen, tall, beautiful with her blonde hair done up in a chignon, wearing a pale green suit and incredibly high heeled shoes. I can still remember the silence in the room! Goodness, fancy having a grown-up sister like that?

In those far off days, once a woman got married, she often couldn't continue in her job. Imagine that? It wasn't like the Dark Ages; IT WAS THE DARK AGES!!

So, Olive could no longer be an AIR hostess but could continue as a Ground hostess and worked in the Airport. This of course didn't apply to her husband. What was the thinking in those days? Honestly, unbelievable! I suppose she was lucky they didn't ask her to give up her job altogether as some other women had to when they got wed.

Anyway, what has this got to do with London? Well, as it was our last year of primary school and Adrienne and I had passed the Qualifying exam and were heading for Lurgan College: as a reward, Adrienne's sister invited her and a friend over to stay with them. Guess who was the lucky friend? Yes, it was me!

Our mothers got together and worked out the logistics and what clothes we would require. I recall new dresses and shorts plus THE latest item of style, plastic macs with hoods! And ours were matching!

As everyone dressed up to fly in aeroplanes in those far off days, we were to wear our new College blazers! Does that seem strange? Not then, in fact it was a way of showing off! We were going to be Grammar School Girls, and everybody needed to know!

My dad came up trumps with a bank bag of sixpences for each of us. In 1956 you could get lots of sweet things for thruppenny bits (a thruppence was three pence), that's what we had normally for holidays, but this was a trip to London, and obviously things would be dearer. Mum and Dad knew this as they had been to London for the Coronation in 1953, no less!

It was our first time on a plane and as we were travelling unaccompanied so the air hostess and the passengers sitting opposite us were very attentive. We had front row seats. Before setting off, a bowl of hard-boiled sweets was passed round. This was to help clear your ears, also a kindly gentleman showed us how to hold our noses and blow: a useful, lifelong piece of knowledge!

Flying for the first time is amazing. Ireland laid out before you with its fifty shades of green is a sight to behold! On landing, so thrilling, the air hostess asked us to wait while all the other passengers disembarked. She led us down the steps and over to a lorry which was taking the luggage to the arrivals lounge. We were loaded into the driver's compartment! Wow! This was something else, we were so high up, I had never been in a lorry before!

The gorgeous Olive and her handsome English husband were waiting for us. We had arrived in England! Hurrah! They whisked us off to their very cute cottage in a Village called George's Green in Buckinghamshire. Their cottage was the Lodge of a rather grand manor house. If you have seen Midsummer Murder, you can picture this scene! An Absolutely, quintessentially, English village!

This was to be an amazing holiday, packed with memories.

Olive took us on the Underground. What a way to travel! We were headed for a visit to the London Palladium, imagine that! It was a variety show with some of the best-known stars of the day: Harry Secombe, Alma Cogan in her gorgeous dresses, Winifred Atwell playing her greatest hits on the piano, Beryl Reid doing her comedy routine, and many more. Best of all we were seeing and hearing them in the flesh! Later in my career when I lived in London, this was my favourite theatre. I see on Goggle that you can buy a video of that 1956 show, but there is nothing to compare to live theatre.

Next big treat was another show at the Empire pool in Wembley where the famous Hollywood actress Esther Williams performed her swimming show including skimming along the water behind a boat! Water skiing! Unheard of then! Crickey! It was all so unbelievable! London was turning out to be the most star studded, magical place!

So many memories come flooding back. They had a television with TWO channels: one had the most entertaining ADVERTS! My favourite programme was I Love Lucy, she was so funny!

The couple, who lived in the beautiful Manor house, were friends of Olive and her husband and they looked after us when they were working. As I recall, they took us to Brighton for a trip to the seaside and even taught us how to play darts in their gorgeous garden.

Adrienne's mother told my mother that this couple weren't actually married! Don't forget this was 1956! Shocking or what!

 They were all so kind and generous to two little girls from N Ireland, though to be fair, we were really well behaved and so excited about everything, they probably enjoyed our company.

It was the holiday of a lifetime! London was my kind of town, to quote Frank Sinatra!

Part 2

George was a Greek Cypriot from Hackney in London who worked one Summer at a restaurant in Great Yarmouth, exactly opposite the café that I worked in. He was related to the owners of the restaurant and his extended family owned several others. How did we meet and why did he become another reason for my fascination with London? Well, read on!

I lived with a family in Regent Road, who also owned various outlets and the owners twin sons, and I often went to the restaurant after work. That's how we got friendly with George! He was great fun and to be honest he was as cute as a button!

Sadly, there was absolutely no chance of romance for any of us as my boss saw himself in Loco Parentis and never let me or the boys out unless we were together! For instance, when some of the girls I worked with were invited to a very well-known pop star's summer house for a party, the boss said I couldn't go as my father wouldn't have let me! Too right he wouldn't! Wise man! The stories they told about the evening were shocking!

However, George did offer to drive me to Lowestoft in his two-tone flash car to meet up with my flat mate who was working there. On the way he said if we were ever in London, he would show us the sights! Well, that was an offer too good not to grab! Wasn't it?

The next New Year's Eve found my flat mate and I on our way to the famous Tottenham Royal dance hall in London, with George and his cousin in his car, which believe it or not had a fully functioning record player in it! Cool or what!

Now you need to understand that in 1963 the Tottenham Royal was one of THE IN PLACES to be because none other than the Dave Clark Five pop group played there! It was to London what the Cavern Club was to Liverpool, though a much bigger and glamourous place than the Cavern Club.

It was so exciting, New Year's Eve! In London! We danced the night away to every up-to-date song in the charts, ending, as it was London, with Knees Up Mother Brown!

What an experience, but it wasn't over yet!

George drove us to Trafalgar Square where we saw revellers jumping in and out of the fountains. Mad or what!

I lived in London for nearly forty years but that was the one and only time I was at Trafalgar Square on New Year's Eve! Thanks George!

True to his word he took us to see all the famous sights of London.

Now, if you have ever been to London at Christmas and New Year you will know what a dazzling experience it is. I realized that this is where I wanted to be!

PART 3

September 1965 found my best friend and I tramping the streets of East Ham trying to find accommodation from a list of addresses given to us by our new employers, Newham Education Authority. I don't know who compiled the list, but every place was already taken! Strange! It couldn't be because we were IRISH, could it? We thought we were British! Every door we knocked on closed behind us or never opened! What were we to do? We started at our new schools as teachers the next day! HELP!

As a last resort we looked at a shop window and there was a card advertising a flat to rent! Hallelujah! This time the wife of the couple who owned the flat was IRISH! HURRAH! and they let us have it there and then!

89 Browning Road, Manor Park London E12! We had done it, we were living and working in London!! We had a roof over our heads!

Mind you, it might have been our first and last night in London as my flat mate could smell gas coming from a cupboard in our bedsitting room! Nightmare! The gas had to be turned off, which meant we couldn't even make a cup of tea! No electric kettles in those days.

Our share of the house was a sitting room with a sofa bed, heated by an open fire, a kitchen with a gas cooker and shared bathroom with a geyser for hot water.

It was very basic, later we had the bedroom when the old Irish couple who had it, moved out/died!

Part 4

I started my teaching career in a very poor part of London's East End. The school was close to West Ham Station and a short underground ride from our nearest station in East Ham, which was handy!

My parents had been to a Garden Party at Buckingham Palace that Summer and decided to check out the school for themselves. This was in retrospect a very sensible thing to do. They met the head, the secretary and some of the staff who promised to look after me. Because of this I was treated really well by them all as they felt responsible for me, plus I was only 20 years old and away from my home in Ireland.

I loved my headteacher, Miss Bryan, she was the kindest person but could be really tough when necessary. The children and parents were extremely rough and sometimes violent. Mind you she had been in the Armed services during the War, had fought Hitler, and didn't stand for any nonsense. Most of the male teachers had also served in the War and trained as teachers afterwards. I was like a child in comparison, just out of the classroom and as green as the grass at home! They were all so supportive, kind and patient.

A young female teacher called Margaret took me under her wing. She was very Scottish, played the piano at assembly, had a great sense of humour and was recently married.

One day I had raging toothache and the head very kindly arranged to take me, after school, to see an emergency dentist. Margaret explained that I would have to pay for dental treatment now that I was an adult and gave me some money. So thoughtful of her.

Driving to the dentist we passed Margaret and an elderly man. Miss Bryan said:

"Oh, look there's Margaret and her husband!"

What a shock! I thought it was her father, he was wearing a gabardine raincoat and a Paddy hat! Surely not! Although her clothes were old fashioned, she was no more than 25 years old, this old guy was older than my dad!

I found out later, when she invited me for tea, that he was forty years older than her, and it must be said an old looking man with old grumpy ways! How did I know his age, well, he had just retired at 65 from the quite glamorous managerial job he had at a large Kensington store. They had met at a Boy Scout Jamboree show, which were very popular in those days, he was the musical director.

Don't judge me, you might have done the same, but when I went to the upstairs bathroom I checked to see if they shared a bed! They did! Boy, was I learning about life!

By the way the dentist was Irish and had trained with my dentist in Ireland! Typical! The long arm of Ireland reaches out, someone always knows someone!

After her husband's retirement, Margaret got a bit restless, and started flirting with the deputy head whose own marriage was on the rocks. How did I know this? Well, she tricked me into going with her to a pub after work, which obviously in his eyes, was a DATE! I was a prize gooseberry! Awkward or what!

Next, he gave me a lift and on the radio was a well-known song of the day with the lyrics,

"I can't let Maggy go!"

He said" Can't let her go! I can't even get hold of her!"

There was no answer to that!

Sadly, her husband died a year or so later. Then her career took off and she became a very successful head teacher.

Some years later I heard about Margaret from a family whose children I taught. In fact, this family were also involved in the

Scout movement and had recently attended her wedding! Looking at the photographs it was a shock to see another elderly man as the groom! They assured me that this old guy was the life and soul of the party, and they made a great couple. Who knew that the Scout movement was a great place for match making across the ages?

Part 5

My first Christmas home should have been a celebration of my twenty-first birthday.

Now, most people in those days got something special for that coming of age or at least a party: I got a pregnant sister to take back to London!

Yes, while I had been away, my older sister realized she was pregnant to a boyfriend who, although on paper, had seemed at least a six out of ten, was now a big fat zero and nowhere to be seen!

Apparently, a discussion among the family members had reached the conclusion that I, being in London, was best placed to take my sister and her problem back with me.

What they hadn't taken into consideration was that I shared a cold-water bedsit, with a pull-down sofa bed, with my flat mate. We could have been thrown out of our accommodation on a week's notice for overcrowding and we had really demanding jobs which were at that time badly paid.

Luck was on our side. I phoned my landlady and explained that my sister needed to come over for a limited period: she was very understanding and raised the rent!

My flat mate was super supportive and backed me up all the way. I could never have coped without her. I would like to take this opportunity to thank her on behalf of our entire family for being the truly good humoured, discreet friend she always has been, at a very difficult time in our family history.

The first thing my sister and I did was queue up at the January sales and buy a single bed plus blankets and sheets which fitted into our bedsit.

Youth was on our side, and we had plenty of laughs. My sister had lived in France for a year and was an excellent cook and housekeeper. The three of us got on really well.

My sister was booked into a mother and baby home in Walthamstow, a couple of bus rides from us. Nowadays, these homes have had a really bad press, but in my memory, they were a sanctuary for girls and their families. Yes, the girls had to help keep the place clean, but I visited twice a week, and my sister was well cared for plus all the girls were in a similar boat, so they had lots in common.

My mother came over for the birth and fell completely in love with the baby, so the solution was that they all return to Ireland when all the boxes were ticked. My sister came back to live with us for a few more weeks till everything was sorted out on both sides of the Irish sea.

Eventually, my parents decided to legally adopt the child themselves to ensure his future security and raise him as their own son. They were truly amazing! My sister was thus "free" to restart her life.

Part 6

I loved the atmosphere of the East End of London, no wonder it inspired Dickens with its mix of cultures and all the ducking and diving that goes on, the great sense of humour and the constant scenarios. It was not dull living at 89 Browning Road! In fact, it was always in vivid moving colour!

Which story would you like to hear?

The night we got raided by the Drug Squad? We demanded an apology from the police as advised by our union.

The odd-looking English insects which turned out to be bedbugs infesting our flat which nearly got us kicked out for reporting this to the authorities who then found lack of safety measures in our house. The landlord was not amused to say the least.

The couple with a baby, who lived downstairs, and he turned out to be a bigamist whose first family lived a mile away?

The baby left on our neighbour's doorstep with a note saying, "This is your husband's!"

The corner shop assistant who invited me to her house full of "HOOKY" goods for sale. I admit I bought a dress!

The New Zealand prostitute who moved in downstairs and had the same name as me? When a male came to the door she asked if he wanted Kiwi Helen or the Teacher Helen. I had a picture of myself standing at the top of the stairs in a gown and mortar board and carrying a cane! God preserve us! I demanded a secure door between us, didn't get it!

When they found out we were teachers, East End men often treated us with respect and called us "MISS" and told us sad tales of lost chances at further education because of the needs of their families. They ended up working at the docks as did our landlord who got up really early, had an Austin 1100, and took in Irish workmen and owned his house and ours, a hardworking man.

So, it was a big surprise when he was arrested and sentenced to nine months in jail for his part in a million pounds of fraud at the docks! It was all over the local paper. What a shock!

When I went to pay the rent that week, his wife asked my advice on the best way to illegally send tobacco to a prisoner. She had some wrapped in silver foil. Now, sadly they never covered that particular skill at any of the teacher's courses I had attended so I wasn't much help.

Amazingly, a few weeks later, he was standing outside his gate as free as a bird!

Apparently, his very expensive brief had been able to prove that the judge had led the jury! "You will find this man guilty!" roared the Judge to the intimidated twelve and it cost £500 pounds every time his expensive lawyer stood up to defend him. Money well spent! Who knew he had that kind of cash? That was another trait of Eastenders, they often told you more than you needed or wanted to know.

All of this had repercussions for me. A new dawn was breaking in my landlord's family life. No longer was he getting up early to work at the docks. he purchased a local Motel, replaced the Austin 1100 with a top of the range Bentley and his wife and child were decked out in furs and diamonds. In fact, he advised me that if I had a spare hundred pounds, he could help me buy a diamond ring made by his contact in Hatton Garden. A hundred pounds to spare! What! Why would I want to do that?

The biggest repercussion for me was when he came to tell me that he was selling his house and ours. I had a new flat mate by now, my faithful friend had run off with a Scotsman a couple of years before. To be fair, he had never raised the rent since my sister's time, and he was now offering me the first opportunity to buy the house for £4000 or half for £2000. I knew neither my flat mate or I would be able or want to buy the house, though it would have been a fantastic investment. It just wasn't on our radar; I did know that the newlyweds who had recently moved in downstairs were really keen to buy it. So, it was a no brainer, my days at 89 were over and we moved on.

Afternoon Tea with an Eskimo

"Miss, can I have a little chat with you?

The Mother of one of my pupils was looking at me with smiling anticipation. She had come up to my classroom when picking up her children at the end of the school day.

It was Marta's mother, a lovely Swedish girl, who was always ready to help with coming on school trips or any other requests we made of parents. Her two little daughters were delightful, so I wasn't expecting this to be a difficult situation.

Marta's mother and I often had "little chats" as Primary School teachers often have with Mother's who feel a bit lonely. Mums frequently confided in me, possibly because I had taught at this school in London's East End for several years and my own daughter had been a pupil.

She entered the classroom on her own, leaving the two girls outside in the corridor. I offered her a seat at one of the tables and she began her story.

Apparently, she had been adopted by and brought up in Sweden by a Swedish couple who had been very good parents to her. However, not unusually, she had always wanted to find her birth mother ever since she had her own children.

Now, at last she had been successful and had discovered that her biological mother was an "Eskimo". As in many countries, supposedly well-meaning powers that be decided that the offspring of "native" tribes would make better citizens if they were taken and raised by "civilized" families! They would be less trouble later on if they learned how to be, in this case "Good little Swedes".

I was touched that she wanted to share this information with me but even more surprised when, not only did she tell me that, "the little Eskimo" as she called her, was due to visit shortly but that she wanted me to come and have afternoon tea with them!

Over my years in the East End of London, I had the pleasure of teaching children from all over the world and found that certain cultures respected teachers highly and it was a sign of personal success and prestige if their child's teacher visited their home. Obviously, one had to treat these requests with diplomacy and be aware that certain rituals may need to be followed. Anything might be possible!

On one occasion I was invited for lunch to the home and at the insistence of a mature student who was with me for a few days. As she was of Asian descent, I was looking forward to something delicious to eat but was really disappointed when she opened a tin of baked beans, and we had them on toast!

An Asian family whose children I had taught and again whose mother was a great support to me, invited my whole family to their house for an evening meal near the end of term in July.

Nothing was too much trouble. She had even cooked a roast chicken with all the trimmings in case we didn't like the array of delicious Asian dishes. What a feast! During the meal the father and sons went off discreetly to pray.

The family were so proud of their beautiful home and particularly pointed out the banister rails which the grandfather had carved. The most surprising part of the evening was when we were taken to a bedroom where we were introduced to Granny and Grandad who were tucked up in bed, wide awake, as anyone would be on a sunny summer's evening! Strange or what?

A couple of weeks later I went home with Marta and her sister: they lived just round the corner from the school.

There at a table in the living room, set out for afternoon tea, was a beaming little lady with very brightly coloured cheeks and in traditional dress. Marta's mother proudly introduced me to "The little Eskimo". I never found out what her name was, and it was too early to be introduced as Mum.

She seemed delighted with everything and everybody. It was a memorable experience and though no one could speak her language we smiled and clapped when a special Homemade cake was produced and made ourselves understood as best, we could.

To be honest, the whole family looked at each other in a state of bewilderment.

Marta's mother was very happy that she had met up with her own mother, but grateful to the family who had raised her and helped her make this connection possible. Sadly, there wasn't much further exchange after this visit, as often when children are removed from their natural environment, they have little in common with the way of life of their natural parents.

I felt really privileged to have been part of that special occasion and all these years later I can still picture and feel the warmth of my only afternoon tea with an Eskimo and her family!

School Trips

Have you ever visited the Isle of Wight? It is a great place for a holiday. I have been fortunate to have spent two family holidays there, but my most vivid memories are of SEVEN school trips in the 1990's.

Believe me, any teachers who volunteer to organize school trips where they are solely responsible for a large group of pupils, night and day, deserve a medal! Parents! Never take these heroes for granted!

The pupils of our large Primary School lived fairly comfortable lives in the East London Borough of Redbridge, coming from a mixture of races and backgrounds. The inhabitants of East London Boroughs are always changing depending on what is going on in the world. Suffice to say we were a multicultural school with parents who wanted the best for their children.

Traditionally the school's oldest pupils took trips Swanage in Dorset, but we decided to take all of the children to a new venue, Little Canada in Fishbourne, Isle of Wight.

When the head teacher and I visited the site with its log cabins set among trees next to Wooton Creek with a programme of activities suitable for all and within easy reach of the famous places to visit it was a done deal once I had checked the safety measures.

Who wouldn't want to live in a log cabin set among trees with a Creek on your doorstep and a full timetable of events. Plus, you would get there by ferry boat! Yeah!

When we put the idea to our 10/11-year-olds and their parents the answer was overwhelming YES! When do we go?

The first year we took just over a hundred children and nine staff including a pupil with spina bifida. Of course, we were not the only school at the site, but we were the biggest by far. We also had the use of two coaches and the drivers.

The children were allocated their log cabins, usually six to a room, and were divided into groups of around twelve with a member of staff in charge of them but NOT sharing the cabin! This was a big change for them all, learning to share a small space with bunk beds and a bathroom.

I was overall in charge, but I did bring the deputy head with me who, although not always a team player, had the great gift of being a natural disciplinarian plus he kept them busy with lots of opportunities to play ball games.

I could tell you lots of stories about our visits but am going to choose my favourite.

Very often the children would respond to being away from home in a variety of ways and in this case, it was for the better.

Mohammad was from Somalia where a civil war was tearing the communities apart. We had children from both sides of the divide. He was brought to school with other children by "Uncle" who seemed to be responsible for them. Certainly, if needed, he was the go-to adult who had some understanding of English.

Mohammad was a difficult, resentful pupil, the one I chose to sit right in front of my desk to ensure full concentration!

It is often said that Muslim boys, because of their culture have little respect for women but I have had a lot of experience with Pupils from all sorts of cultures and have found that there are boys and girls who show little respect for their teachers or sadly their parents. Sometimes it is a clash of personalities and Mohammad, and I clashed several times. One day he had been in a bad mood all day when he decided to shake his cartridge pen so violently that the ink flew out onto my skirt. I could be pushed too far and could get angry, so I reported his actions to "Uncle" who was most apologetic and offered to pay for the skirt to be cleaned.

The next day, Mohammad came to school obviously suffering the effects of a beating but with a better attitude to lessons!

All of our pupils loved the Isle of Wight. They were excited by the ferry ride and the beautiful surroundings. Many encouraged their parents to take family holidays there. Some fantasized about living there!

Mohammad was a complete revelation away from home, such a different child. He stayed by my side during all the trips out, helping me on and off boat trips, up and down steps and making sure I was always comfortable. What a change!

The night before we left, he spoke to me privately and asked if, during our journey back on the ferry, he could buy me a cup of tea and a cake, just the two of us! He must have seen other people doing this on the way over plus he must have worked out how much it would cost and kept that amount by. Normally we never purchased anything on the ferry, only at the coach stop.

It was a strange request, afternoon tea on the ferry, very civilized!

Fortunately, all the pupils were occupied and looked after while Mohammad and I took tea together in the cafeteria. Bless him, he made polite conversation and had impeccable manners! The ferry journey doesn't take very long, so by the time we had finished it was time to disembark.

I often wonder if Mohammed had wanted to reinact a scene from a film or TV programme but it is a very sweet memory, sipping tea and sampling cake with a charming companion.

We only had a few weeks of the school year left before these pupils moved on to Secondary school.

It was years later that out of the blue, Mohammad FOUND me on Facebook. He was training to be a DOCTOR at a medical College in Rumania! I was able to see photos of him and several others studying in a room with bunk beds and laptops! My favourite photo was one where he was dressed for what was obviously a formal dinner, he was looking very dapper.

Then just as suddenly he was no longer on Facebook!

Hopefully, he became a doctor and fulfilled his potential. You never know he may well be working on the Isle of Wight!

My Father

The man who invented himself

Many people search for their ancestry, get their DNA tested, hoping to find some interesting people in their past. Yes, even though I have had my DNA tested, I have always believed that down through the ages on my Paternal side, no one could be more interesting than my own father.

If you had met my father, say around 1970, you would have seen a well-dressed, good-looking man of nearly sixty, speaking with a cultured Northern Ireland burr. His grey eyes sparkled when he laughed or talked about his beloved country. Dad was, at that time, a Unionist MP for Stormont. He represented North Armagh until Stormont was closed down in 1972 during the Troubles. Being an MP was to be the pinnacle of his political career but not the end of it.

As part of his role in a Unionist government, he was selected to the Commonwealth committee of the Westminster Government, representing N Ireland. I had the privilege of meeting up with him in London at a Commonwealth conference where he enjoyed the company of members from around the world. This environment was where he was totally comfortable, listening to others and selling Northern Ireland to everybody and everybody.

How did he become this erudite politician, consumed by endless energy and ambition? Where did it all start?

RJ as he was known, was the eldest child born in November 1911, into an Ulster Scots family, farming the fertile land of the Lower Bann valley. He had a sister and a brother, his parents were typical of that era, having to wait to be married until the Matriarch died. His Grandmother's uncle had bought the farm for her and her infant son when her Scottish husband became ill and died while in his thirties. She was not a woman to share the work or home with another female, so his parents were in their late thirties when he was born.

His family were hard working, God fearing, honest farmers, with no greater ambitions other than to make their farms as prosperous as possible and to keep out of debt.

Now as the eldest son, RJ would have traditionally inherited the farm. However, he turned out to be academically very bright, winning a place at Ballycastle High School and achieving top marks at Drumreagh Presbyterian Sabbath School exams, so the family's highest ambition for his future was to try to pass the Belfast Bank exam!

In those days, bank clerks were not allowed to work in their own towns for obvious reasons of privacy, so RJ was posted to Londonderry. This must have been so exciting as the Belfast bank was an imposing building in Guildhall Square, right in the centre of the bustling city! I often feel his presence when I visit Londonderry and picture this young man straight off the farm, straight backed, in a well-cut suit, shoes well shined, his very black hair slicked back and the latest style of moustache on his upper lip.

He told me that the minister of one of the Presbyterian Churches had been contacted by his own minister and welcomed him into the church where he soon was helping to run their Boys' Brigade.

 One of his jobs, as a junior bank clerk, was to go in a taxi once a week and collect the pennies from the Gas Board which people had put into their Gas meters. Quite a responsibility and possibly dangerous!

Onwards and upwards! Next, he was sent to Belfast where he realized that learning to drive might be a useful skill. So, he set about teaching himself, in a field, in a van, borrowed from his landlord. All young bank clerks had to live in accommodation approved by the Bank, for reasons of security and safety.

By the time he met our mother in 1937, he was now a senior bank clerk in the Portadown branch of the Belfast Bank, 25 years old and had changed his affiliation from Presbyterianism to the Baptist Church where he was training to be a preacher. I have his Bible which has pages in it to make notes for sermons. He obviously took this very seriously.

Somewhere along the way, he had shed his Antrim Ulster Scot's accent and learned about etiquette, manners, getting suits tailored and collars and shirts laundered. The new RJ was well on his way!

Our Mother's father had sadly died but had been the owner of the local Foundry. All the family had all been left shares in the will and her young brother was destined to take over. The family belonged to the Brethren sect, as did many of the owners of companies and the very important linen trade in that town. All very rich and important people. As a bank clerk, RJ knew who had money and how much!

Spotting our mother driving round the town (a rarity then), in the large family car, he determined to find out more about her and her background.

Always a charmer, he asked his very respectable land lady to invite our mother for afternoon tea to his very respectable dwellings. There was nowhere they would have crossed paths except in the bank as Brethren did not mix with others socially, they spent their time exclusively with other members of the sect.

Our Mother was desperate to escape the strictures of her religion and saw in this young man her way out, if it was possible. Probably, had her father still been alive, it would have been a lost cause, but RJ managed to charm our grandmother and eventually the romance proceeded to the point where she allowed the wedding reception to be held in her garden! It was a very stylish affair, though the ceremony had to take place in Lurgan Baptist Church where our father was a member at that time.

RJ was moving ever upwards!

As newlyweds, they began their married life as tenants of a very wealthy linen baron whose lifestyle, as lord of the manor, began a new ambition in his life. Could this be his future?

Sadly, this man's influence was to cause major problems. One of my father's greatest faults all through his life was to be blinded by people of a higher social level and put his trust in them.

It is not always known that there was no conscription in Northern Ireland during World War 2 as in the rest of the UK. Therefore, everyone who joined the services was a volunteer. However, the province needed protection so RJ joined the local Home Guard of the British Army and quickly rose to the rank of Captain.

Encouraged by the new influences in his life, RJ took the huge step of leaving the bank and plunging headlong into a business venture. The idea of a Dairy which provided all milk products was brilliant and ahead of his time. With his background in farming and the promises of backing from his mentors this unfortunately led to an overestimation of his own business acumen, something which would recur time and again.

Sadly, for our family it was a financial disaster, but it made a fortune for someone else!

With a growing family to support the idea of emigration to Canada seemed a solution for a while. However, this was a non-starter.

With the help of my mother's family the couple were able to purchase a detached chalet bungalow in a pleasant area of Lurgan. RJ found himself a job with a major oil company and this meant dressing in suits and being provided with a company car and a reasonable salary.

RJ was on the rise again.

His time in the Home Guard naturally led to joining the Territorial Army, the prestigious North Irish Horse! Having always been interested in the development of Radio he was put in charge of that section and held onto the rank of Captain. This gave him excellent prestige and the opportunity of new areas to explore.

None of his family had been involved in politics, but with his massive self-belief and training in public speaking during his preacher days plus his army experience, he realized he had what it took to become a politician.

Thus, he set about joining the Ulster Unionist Party which also needed membership of the Orange Order.

Very quickly he stood for election to the local council. Being a natural orator and with his own personal charisma plus the confidence which came from dressing well and being an officer in the Army meant that he had no difficulty in being elected. Certainly, one of his aims was to improve the life of the inhabitants of the town. He was a tireless Councillor who took the time to listen and attend to his constituents.

Politics became an all-consuming force in his life.

Always ambitious for his family he became a Governor at Lurgan College where all his children became pupils and were beginning to show real ability.

Somewhere during his time on Lurgan Council he saw that a large house which had been a former Rectory would be a possible renovation project and a major step up. It had been left derelict for several years but on inspection he could see its potential. Set on three acres of grounds close to the town centre, he set about planning how it could be turned into a beautiful home.

My father could turn his hands to anything, decorating, carpentry, gardening. With our mother's help they planned out how to bring this late Georgian wreck into its former glory both in the house and in the grounds. It became the most amazing home in which to grow up.

My mother loved to play tennis, so we had a grass tennis court. There was a Victorian wall garden already and it became an orchard of apple and pear trees with endless black currant bushes. All great for making jam.

County Armagh is famous as the garden of Northern Ireland and with my father's green fingers he developed the most beautiful flower beds and lawns. There was also a very productive field which produced potatoes, cabbages and cauliflowers. Later our father turned one of the areas into a putting green.

There was also a paddock and, on a whim, for a while, we had a pony to ride. Sadly, as teenagers, we didn't enjoy the amount of work that poor Dolly needed, so it was taken back to its original owner.

With two children at Queen's University, living as landed gentry, my father's cup overflowed when he was voted in as Mayor of the town!

How much further could he go?

The Fifties was a very prosperous time in Northern Ireland with new council houses replacing slums people wanting cars, televisions, all manner of white goods. Businesses were thriving so much so that richer families were buying second homes in popular seaside towns!

A visit to the Ideal Homes exhibition in Belfast inspired RJ to not buy but BUILD his own second home in Portrush! A very modern design, this bungalow had glass walls to enhance the magnificent unrestricted views over the Atlantic Ocean from a site he had chosen in a town he knew very well from his childhood. No half measures with this guy!

Getting together with a builder from Lurgan, they planned out two bungalows on the site RJ had bought. This area would prove to be massively popular both then and in the future!

As fishing was his passion, he also purchased a small cottage in Donegal set in a large number of acres where salmon and trout were plentiful.

Another year as Mayor of Lurgan was to come as was the honour of being awarded the Territorial Decoration for services to the TA. This meant that not only could he have these letters after his name, but he was allowed to use the title of Captain. Also being made a Justice of the Peace, RJ was now Captain Robert James Mitchell TD JP!

Rising ever more, he was chosen as Member of the Northern Ireland Parliament for North Armagh, representing the Ulster Unionist Party. In those days the Government in Stormont was predominately Ulster Unionist with the firebrand Ian Paisley's new party, the Democratic Unionists. All Protestants!

RJ relished his new role, but attitudes were changing, and people were demanding rights that most of us didn't know they had been denied. This led to marches, riots, the British Army being brought in and sadly the deaths of many, many people. The country was totally split, with hatred, mistrust and suspicion being the big winners. Stormont was seen as not representing the citizens and the British Government decided to close it down.

This left RJ and his family in a very dangerous situation. Lurgan was a divided town with two groups of paramilitaries gunning for each other. In the middle was RJ, the hated Unionist representative of an oppressive regime, and to the other side, the Representative of a regime which was seen as caving into the demands of what was now the enemy.

Our beautiful home became the target of both factions and our mother's life was threatened. RJ tried to hold out as long as he could but as the "Troubles" became worse and worse with no end in sight, the family had to move from nightly dangers and attacks to the comparative peace of the second home in Portrush.

Sadly, the locals took delight in stripping the Rectory of anything they could, breaking the windows and ruining the grounds. What should have been a property, worth a fortune to a developer, became a wasteland, virtually worthless!

The cottage and the acres in Donegal had to go as it was in a dangerous area and another financial loss!

For many weaker human beings, all this would have broken a lesser couple than my parents. But there was still life in them both. They began to enjoy their new life in Portrush, RJ kept his ties with the Oil Company and represented the Company Pensioners. He got involved with various entrepreneurs and with his skill and experience as a salesman he made a good living.

However, as a consummate Politician, he soon joined the Local Unionist party and stood for Coleraine council to represent the Skerries area of Portrush. Known as the Captain, RJ became a well-known and respected figure in the area, so much so that when he parted ways with the Unionist Party, he was still voted in by his constituents, standing as an Independent and then as a

Conservative becoming secretary of his local branch. He was on the governing body of the local Primary school and a committee member of Portrush Presbyterian Church. He truly loved being a politician with a passion and belief that Northern Ireland was the best place to live. Everywhere he went he tried to sell it to any captive audience.

When the Lottery became popular, RJ, though brought up to stay clear of gambling, regularly tried his luck, believing that as the money was used for charity, it was actually in a good cause.

He told me his plans for when the big win would come:

He would buy a Rolls Royce

Employ a Chauffeur ...He actually had someone in mind, ever hopeful!

He would pay off all our mortgages.

Always an optimist! Only a heart attack could quench that energy.

Now, RJ was no saint, he had lots of faults, but it can't be denied that he was a very interesting man, using his given talents to turn the boy of the farm into a politician who could hold his own with anyone, rich or poor, important or insignificant.

I am proud to call him my father.

Printed by Amazon Italia Logistica S.r.l.
Torrazza Piemonte (TO), Italy